A WITCH'S GARDEN

Jenny's twelfth summer turned out to be the most eventful one she'd ever had. Until then, Clover Lake had seemed a perfect place to live. Now Jenny wasn't sure. It was a "club," for members only, and the Membership Committee was narrow-minded and bigoted. Jenny's best friend had just moved away with her family because of this, and, in a fit of anger and frustration at their stupidity, Jenny put a childish curse on the committee. Then a new family arrived. Jenny found young Mrs. Matthews as strange as she was interesting and friendly. She kept a rat for a pet and filled her garden with hemlock, wolfbane, and other poisonous plants. And no sooner did she learn of Jenny's dislike for the Membership Committee than little mishaps began to plague its members—amusing at first, then growing more serious until Jenny was frightened. What if Mrs. Matthews were a witch? Should Jenny try to exorcise her?

Jenny's decision and its results are at the heart of this sometimes funny, always unexpected, and altogether convincing book that will delight young readers right to its surprise ending.

Weekly Reader Books presents

MIRIAM YOUNG

Illustrated by Charles Robinson

A MARGARET K. MC ELDERRY BOOK

ATHENEUM 1976 NEW YORK

FOR LORI

Clover Lake exists nowhere but in the author's mind. The characters in this story are fictional, as are the incidents in it—excepting caterpillar plagues and dams breaking, which happen everywhere. Any resemblance to persons living or dead, or actual events, is purely coincidental.

Library of Congress catalog card number 72–85922
ISBN *0–689–30323–8*
Published simultaneously in Canada by
McClelland & Stewart, Ltd.
Manufactured in the United States of America

This book is a presentation of
Weekly Reader Books.
Weekly Reader Books offers
book clubs for children from
preschool to young adulthood. All
quality hardcover books are selected
by a distinguished Weekly Reader
Selection Board.

For further information write to:
Weekly Reader Books
1250 Fairwood Ave.
Columbus, Ohio 43216

A WITCH'S GARDEN

ONE

At first I thought of violent deaths. Then of slow, torturous ones, like being eaten by tiny red ants. Finally, I decided that death—lying in some peaceful cemetery—was too good for him.

I'm speaking of Russell Pettit. Thanks to him, I am losing my three best friends at one blow: Diane Holcombe, whom I've known since kindergarten, her brother Richard, and Paul Green, the boy I most admire at school.

I keep wondering if I'll ever see them again. I'm sure they won't come back here, any of them, after what's happened. And, personal feelings aside, it's the injustice of the thing that infuriates me.

We live in a place called *Clover Lake Club—Mem-*

bers Only, according to the signs. That means some people are good enough to live here and others aren't. Who decides? The Membership Committee, which consists of Russell Pettit, chairman, and four yes-men. They said, "No," when the Greens wanted to rent the Holcombes' house for the summer. The Holcombes were indignant. They'd been friends with the Greens for years.

Why were the Greens rejected? Mrs. Green is sweet and quiet. Paul is one of the smartest boys in my class. Mr. Green is a violinist with the Philharmonic—and Jewish.

Oh, yes: there is a law that no one can refuse to sell or rent a house on the basis of color, race, or religion. But this is a club. Private clubs can select their members. So the Greens were given some phony excuse, and the Holcombes put their house up for sale. They didn't want anything more to do with Clover Lake. They're building a place in Maine. That's why I was furious.

The night of the Annual Meeting I went to the clubhouse with my parents on the pretext of taking an evening swim at the beach. Mr. Pettit was to give his report, and I wanted to see if he'd have guts enough to state the real reason for turning the Greens down.

We all three sighed as we passed the Holcombes' house on the fork of the road. It's an unusual place, with two faces, like a coin. In front, its dark gray frame is brightened by window boxes planted with geraniums.

The other side, the one we see from our road, has a spooky look, especially at dusk when its steep roof and octagonal tower stand in black silhouette against the sky.

Tonight, however, the whole house was brightly lighted. The Holcombes were packing. Someone new would be living there in the future—some dull, ordinary family of whom Mr. Pettit and his gang would approve. I kicked a stone in the road. I already felt desolate and forsaken.

"There's no need to hate the whole world, Jenny," Mother said.

"I'm supposed to love everybody, I suppose? Even bigots?"

"Not necessarily. But hating doesn't accomplish anything."

If I had known what was going to happen I might have said, "That's what *you* think."

Cars passed us on the road—some new, some old, for in spite of its exclusive attitude, this is a middle-class community. Some of the men are executives, but others are carpenters or plumbers. And lots of the women work, too.

Mr. and Mrs. Pettit waved as they drove by. He's a retired salesman. She's very pleasant, and he likes to laugh and joke. He'd probably be amazed to know that one person, at least, considers him a minor Hitler.

Near the mail boxes some scraps of paper and a beer

can lay on the ground. Daddy went toward them, remarking about litter spoiling the beauty of the countryside. But Mother got there first. "It's good for my waistline," she said.

We went on to the clubhouse. My parents went inside. I went around to the porch. Clover Lake is small, only a mile around, but on summer days, when the sky is blue and the water still and the trees stand like silent green guardians, it's almost too pretty to be real. I feel sorry for people who have to move away. Like the Holcombes.

It was June. One of those evenings when the air is so soft you want to throw your arms around a tree. It was a shame to spend it spying, but it couldn't be helped. I sat near an open window, half listening, until Mr. Pettit was asked for his report.

"The Membership Committee has been exceptionally active this past year, thanks to IBM," he said. "Those initials stand for I've Been Moved. Ha, ha."

A joke ten years old is just his style. He laughed immoderately, and after mentioning the new club members who had been accepted during the year, he came to the Greens.

"They may be very fine people. I'm sure they are! But we on the committee just felt they wouldn't fit in. We're a pretty nice bunch, here, if I do say so. We're all Christians and . . ."

"Drop dead," I muttered.

". . . we don't want anything to spoil . . ." His

voice broke off. Russell Pettit's face turned purple under his white hair. There was a crash as a chair overturned, and he fell. Then a hush, and someone was bending over him to whisper, "He's gone."

But only in my imagination, alas. Actually, Mr. Pettit was going on, healthy and hearty as ever. After explaining that one of his "crew," Mr. Whipple, was in the hospital, he called on other members of his committee to present the points they had considered.

Mr. Hillyer stood up. He teaches math at our high school, and all the girls are in love with him.

"I'd like to say that I have nothing, personally, against the Greens. I play golf with Mort Green, and he's as nice a guy as you'd want to meet. But we've got to remember that once we open the doors . . . well, let one in, and we'll be overrun with them."

You'd have thought he was talking about termites. Handsome is as handsome does, I said to myself.

Mrs. Parsons was the next member of the committee to speak. She's from Mississippi and is usually sparkling with laughter. Tonight she was serious.

"I just want to say one thing: once we let *them* in, you know what will happen *next.* I'm not prejudiced, but you let these Northern Nigrahs into a white community, and they get so biggity it's disgusting."

A third member stood up—Mrs. Orton. I don't know where she's from, but she has a quiet way of speaking that makes you listen. "Regardless of our individual feelings about minorities, we've got to be realistic. We know what will happen to property values if this place becomes really unrestricted."

Mrs. Orton is in Real Estate, so I guess she knows.

Mr. Hillyer spoke again. "Another thing we have to consider is their relatives. We don't know what *they'd* be like. I'm sure you all know what I mean."

His wife, Lisa, jumped up. "I'm speaking out of turn because I'm not on the committee, but Bill and I don't agree on this matter at all. I say that if people are nice themselves, like the Greens, we shouldn't worry about their relatives. After all, you admitted me, and you don't know what my relatives are like."

Everyone laughed. Daddy flashed her an admiring look and stood up, intending to say he agreed, I'm sure, but Mrs. Parsons was already speaking.

"Isn't it the *truth!*" she laughed. "I've got a couple of second cousins I wouldn't want *any*body to see!"

People laughed until Mr. Walsh, the president, rapped with his gavel. Mr. Pettit had an answer for Lisa Hillyer.

"What we had in mind, Lisa, was our little beach here. You wouldn't want it swarming with a lot of . . . well, I don't have to draw a picture. We all know what Miami Beach looks like. But actually," he went on in his big, warm voice, "the main thing is, if people aren't our kind, they wouldn't be happy here."

Garbage! I hated them all. I wanted to run away—almost. I almost hated Clover Lake. I was ashamed of living in such a place. I left the porch, stamped through the sand, crossed the wooden bridge over the dam, and went scuffling through the knoll.

Peering through the dusk to avoid poison ivy, I saw a scattering of the weed called devil's beard, growing in a circle near an old yew tree. I hadn't thought of it in years, but when we were little, we used to believe that if you wished on that weed, the devil himself would answer.

It was nonsense, of course, and I had no wishes. But I had to vent my anger somehow. I snatched up a weed by its blood red stem. "Damn Russell Pettit! Damn the whole committee!"

TWO

MY FATHER, STERLING HENDERSON, is a quiet man. He wears quiet ties and quiet shirts and is witty in a quiet way. He looks like a professor, and that is what he is. He teaches History of Art at the University. In the summer he has a morning class tutoring.

Mother works in an antique shop. She's interested in ballet, music, handicrafts, and almost everything but housework. She likes to joke and is generally lighthearted, but this morning she was gloomy.

I couldn't blame her. We'd all been at the Holcombes' the night before, saying good-by. It was depressing to see the house I knew so well stripped of rugs and furniture and filled with trunks and cartons.

"I can't forgive Mary for leaving," Mother mourned

at breakfast. "Who am I going to talk to?"

Mother and Mrs. Holcombe had a lot in common; they were always visiting back and forth.

"How about me?" I said. "Do you know I'm the only twelve-year-old here? This place is just one giant kindergarten!"

There are a few older kids who go away to college, enough boys for a Little League team, and the rest are babies. There's always been just Diane and Richie Holcombe, my age, and Paul Green, when he came to visit. Also Shawn Denihee, but he goes to private school now.

"Sometimes," Mother sighed, "I'd like to get away from here myself. But where would we ever find another place on the water?"

They bought this place years ago when prices were low. Daddy says you'd have to be rich to find waterfront property anywhere now. We're just lucky. Our house is smallish, but it has a wonderful view. The lawn slopes down in a green curve to the lake. Here, where lawn and water meet, the tumbled rocks of an old stone wall are grown over with wild forget-me-nots. On both sides of our land weeping willows dip feathery fronds to touch their own reflections.

"I'd die if we ever had to leave," I said. Then, thinking of Diane, who enjoyed the lake as much as I, I felt resentful of the Membership Committee again.

"Wouldn't you hate having somebody say you were biggity, just because you wanted to live like other people do?"

“Sally Lou is really a very nice person. And her children are so well brought up!”

Mother’s always rushing to someone’s defense as if she were afraid of getting a demerit for being critical. I put on my bathing suit and headed for the beach, going the long way around to avoid passing the Holcombes’ house. It had been bad enough seeing it the night before.

“You’ll have to come stay with us in Maine,” Diane had said. But her mother had pointed out that at present they had no room. They were renting a mobile home while their house was being built. “Well, next year you’ll have to come up for a month anyway.”

Fine, I thought. But how will I get through *this* summer?

Diane wasn’t as devastated as I. And no wonder. She’d be in a new world. Mine would be the same old world—with a hole in it. If I thought about it too much, I’d feel like crying. So I let my anger grow. I had to fill that empty space somehow.

I like swimming in the morning. Most of the mothers, with their babies, don’t come till afternoon when their housework is done. The beach was almost deserted. I swam to the float and back a few times and then stretched out on a bench to bake. Later, when I was half-asleep, something tapped my bare foot.

“Hello, there!” It was Mrs. Pettit. “I wouldn’t sleep in the sun if I were you, dear. You can get a bad burn.”

I never burn; I just get tan. But she has white hair

and one of those pink-and-white complexions that blister.

"I was just passing and saw someone lying here. I'm lucky to find you. Would you do me a favor and give this to your father?" She held out a sheet of paper. "Thank you, dear. Just have him initial this after the meeting."

"What meeting? There just *was* one."

She gave a tinkling laugh. I've noticed that women her age laugh all the time, whether something is funny or not. "That was the annual meeting, Jenny. This is a meeting of the Membership Committee. Your father's the new member, you know."

"My father! He's not on *that* committee!"

She laughed again. "He is now. Mr. Whipple has had an operation and is going to stay with his daughter. Your father is taking his place." She waved her car keys and left.

I held the paper from me as if it were tainted. In another moment I was running home, not even noticing the Holcombes' place with its uncurtained windows and deserted terrace. Not *my* father! He wouldn't join the enemy! Mrs. Pettit must be wrong.

The front door slammed behind me.

"Don't slam the door like that, Jenny," Mother called.

"I didn't slam it; the wind did." When the porch door is open, the wind always whips the door closed, catching the window curtain. Mother and Daddy were on the porch painting the porch furniture. Daddy had paint on one of his bushy eyebrows. I waved the paper.

"It's not true, is it, Daddy? You're not going to be on dopey Pettit's committee!"

Daddy said that though he disliked the whole idea of such a committee, he had agreed to serve on it.

"Fink! You let them talk you into it."

Daddy has one trouble: he's too easy-going. He'll do anything to avoid an argument. Now he'd gone into the enemy camp. What good would his vote do? It would be four against one all the time.

"Fine," I said. "Maybe Mr. Pettit will get to be president of the club. Maybe he'll run for governor of the state. He'll probably put segregation back into the schools saying, 'They wouldn't be happy with white children.' "

"Are we going to have some lunch?" Daddy asked amiably.

Mother sighed. She'd rather paint furniture or make curtains or hang wallpaper. She says anything you have to do every day of the week and twice as much on holidays has got to be a bore. Daddy and I think she's a great cook, just the same. "How about you making lunch, Jen? I'm full of paint. Sandwiches and milk will be fine."

I spread bread with mayonnaise, deviled ham, and pickle relish and carried sandwiches and milk to the porch. My question had prompted a discussion of the annual meeting.

"They ought to put Lisa Hillyer on that committee," Mother said. "She's so cute. I love the way she got up and said, 'You don't know anything about my relatives.' That looks good, Jenny."

"She's not really pretty," Daddy said, which didn't seem to relate to the discussion at all. After a moment he added, "As for Sylvia Orton, I don't think she has any convictions. Russell talks in a loud voice, and she goes along with him."

You'd never talk in a loud voice, I wanted to say. You'd let some blow-hard like Mr. Pettit go booming away and convince everybody.

"You should have been here, Jenny," Mother laughed. "You'd have loved what Mr. Pettit said to Daddy. 'You're just the type we want, Sterling,' he said."

I suddenly saw the joke. Daddy *isn't* the type. As I've mentioned, he's a quiet man and very agreeable. He goes out of his way to help people and looks as if he wouldn't say boo to a baby. He looks like another yes-man, but he isn't.

Years ago when my parents first moved here, Daddy raised absolute hell when a Girl Scout troop was not allowed to use the clubhouse because one of the Brownies was black. You may find that unbelievable, and of course it wouldn't happen today; that was twenty years ago.

Daddy lost his fight that time and the troop had to meet elsewhere.

"How could they do that?" I had asked when Daddy first told me about it. "You can't do that to the Girl Scouts."

"They did," he said. "They used the same old words

they're using now. 'We don't want to set a precedent.' But times have changed, thank goodness."

It's true. Several families invite kids from Harlem to spend part of the summer here now, and two black boys from down the road come to play with our Little Leaguers.

When we were eating our sandwiches, Daddy asked Mother to read the paper I'd brought from Mrs. Pettit since his glasses were inside. It was an application for membership. "What's the name of these people?" he asked.

"Matthews. I'll have to give a coffee for her one day soon so she can meet some of the women."

"Soon?" I cried, shocked. "You mean these people are moving right in?" It seemed wrong, somehow. The Holcombes had scarcely got their things out.

"Name of applicant," Mother read, "*Mr. and Mrs. John Matthews. Children's names . . .*"

"Mark and Luke?" Daddy suggested.

"*Niobe and Pookie.*"

"Ni-o-be!" I repeated. "And Pookie! Please. Not while I'm eating. What are they—boys or girls or what?"

"Wife's maiden name, *Meeghan Gitane.*"

"Meeghan! Of all the crazy . . . !"

"I like it," Mother said. "It sounds like a princess in an Irish fairy tale."

"Gitane," Daddy offered, "means 'gypsy' in French." He's taking advanced French from an old Frenchwoman, Madame Vartan, and is really hung up on the language. He even studies it on the train. He loves studying anything. Mother says he'd be happy in a cell if you filled it with books.

"*Employer's name*," Mother read on, "Hm, sounds like an advertising agency. *Frisby*, *Crosby*, *Cunningham and Peters*."

"Sounds like a bunch of rabbits—Flopsy, Mopsy, Cottontail, and Peter," I grumbled.

"Anyway," Mother sighed. "It sounds as if they'd be approved by the committee."

"The devil with the committee!" I threw down my sandwich and looked at my hand. My third finger was still red from the devil's beard weed. It must be a kind of nettle.

THREE

IT WAS ELEVEN O'CLOCK on a Sunday morning a week later. Breakfast was turning into brunch with muffins and jam and the great, enormous *New York Times* weighing down the table.

Mother was looking at fashions in the magazine section. "I'm going on a diet tomorrow," she said, taking another muffin.

Daddy had the art section. "Good. That's when everybody goes on a diet—tomorrow." He glanced at his watch. "Don't let me forget that meeting. It's at one."

I groaned. Daddy was going to the clubhouse to meet the Matthews with the rest of the Membership Committee.

"If you keep scowling like that, Jenny," Mother said,

"you're going to have a permanent line between your eyebrows."

Daddy has a line between *his* eyebrows, and it just makes him look thoughtful. I've noticed that the men in advertisements are always scowling, while the women all look serene and smiling. It's not fair. I can never be a model, anyway; you've got to be tall and beautiful. I might as well frown.

"I guess I'll go down to the beach when Daddy goes."

I had no intention of going swimming. I wanted to get a look at the new people. There was just a chance that the kids might be my age and fun, in spite of their crazy names. I ate another muffin.

Mother had started the crossword puzzle. "Sterling, what's 'stale' in French. Six letters."

"*Rassis*," Daddy said promptly. He knows every word of the language, even slang. He spelled it for her.

"*Rassis*. That doesn't look French, it looks Egyptian. But it fits. Thanks."

I put on my bathing suit, and at twelve forty-five Daddy and I walked to the clubhouse. It takes three minutes, but he likes to be prompt. The porch was jammed with mothers and babies, so I slipped into the card room. It has two doors—one leading to the stairs, the other to the main room. Bridge chairs were lined against the wall under framed photographs of club officers. I set one of them between the two doors where I'd be able to see both ways, sat down, and opened a book I'd brought along, hoping not to be noticed.

Mrs. Orton came first and went right into the main room. Then Mrs. Parsons. She was wearing white slacks and looked nice, as usual. She peeked into the card room. "Hi! Is that new?" she asked, meaning my old bathing suit. "It's precious!"

"It's two years old," I muttered, though it's hard not to respond to someone who's so friendly.

Mr. Hillyer came bounding up the stairs two at a time. He went on without seeing me, and I was glad. If he smiled at me, I know I'd have to smile back. He really is nice looking.

Moments later, a voice boomed from the bottom of the stairs, "Anybody home?" The Chairman had arrived. The stairs creaked under his weight, and he joined the others.

"Nobody here but us chickens, eh? Ha ha. How are you, Sylvia? Afternoon, Sally Lou. Hello, Bill. Glad to have you with us, Sterling. Welcome aboard. I hope the Matthews aren't lost. They're from Greenwich Village. I'm throwing that in for what it's worth. Ah, here they are now."

A car door slammed. The screen door gave its twanging yawn. Mr. Pettit went to the landing.

"Well, well, well! Right on time. Come on up, folks. Our main room is up here. Locker rooms and kitchen down there. Come up and meet a few of your neighbors."

I strained to see past Mr. Pettit's bulk as he shook hands with the newcomers.

"Mr. Matthews? Glad to meet you. I'm Russell

Pettit. And who is this lovely young lady with you—your *daughter?*" From his fatuous tone it was obvious that he would have said the same thing if she had been sixty. At last he moved aside. Mr. Matthews was of slight build with sandy-gray hair. The same type as Daddy. Mrs. Matthews had gone ahead. Determined to get a look at her, I went to stand in the doorway, hoping no one would object.

No fear. They couldn't spare a glance. They were all too busy looking at Mrs. Matthews. I did some staring myself. In spite of the warm June day, she was wearing a dress of orange wool with a black patent leather belt and bag and knee-high boots to match. She looked like someone on the cover of a fashion magazine. Her long blond hair was drawn back with a black velvet ribbon, and she wore no jewelry except for a black pin the shape of a caterpillar.

Fashion plate, I thought scornfully. Who needs her? She was too young to have children my age and too young to be company for Mother.

But if I was disappointed, the men were captivated. They were all laughing in a silly way, even my father, and practically knocking each other over trying to offer her a chair.

Mrs. Matthews remained standing, looking around the room, which was still decorated with branches and flowers from the dance they'd had the night before. She glanced at the blossoming boughs hung from the overhead beams.

"I see you celebrate Midsummer's Eve." Her voice was low and husky.

Two or three people answered at once, telling her there had just been a dance but that several parties and dinners were held during the year. There was a lot of small talk, and finally Mr. Pettit suggested they get down to business.

"The purpose of this meeting is just to get acquainted and give you any information you might need," he said, skirting the truth. "I believe your application said you had two children?"

"Yes, two. Is that all right?" Mrs. Matthews asked in an eager, hopeful way that made everyone laugh.

Mrs. Orton asked how old they were.

"Niobe is nine, and Pookie has just turned four," Mr. Matthews said, and looked at his wife adoringly as if no one else had ever done anything as clever as to produce them.

Mrs. Parsons told them about the schools and school buses and began to tell them where the churches of different denominations were located.

"Don't forget the *Temple*," Mr. Pettit broke in with a grin. "They might want to know how to find the Temple, ha ha!"

Big joke. Daddy scowled. The Matthews looked puzzled. Mr. Hillyer coughed, Mrs. Orton looked at her hands, and Mrs. Parsons, the only one to smile, gave Mr. Pettit a playful slap. After which she started her recitation again. This time Mr. Matthews interrupted.

"We don't go to church." He smiled pleasantly. "Thanks, anyway."

Mrs. Matthews crossed her knees. "They wouldn't let me in," she said in her husky voice.

"Come, now," Mr. Pettit boomed. "All the girls are

wearing short skirts these days." He shook his head in mock disapproval. "I tell you, it's terrible. I'm going to have to get new glasses so I don't miss anything!" He burst out laughing.

Mrs. Orton's assignment was to tell about rubbish collection and supermarkets; Mr. Hillyer's about swimming and skating and the water supply. Daddy told about the roads—their maintenance, snow removal, etc. Mr. Pettit wound up by giving the club rules.

"No one allowed in the main room here in a wet bathing suit—or without one, ha ha. No horses. No livestock. But I don't suppose you people kept chickens down in the city. Dogs and cats, yes, as many as you like. There must be as many dogs here as there are youngsters. And the place is overrun with cats."

"How about rats?" Mrs. Matthews asked.

He assured her there were none that he knew of.

"I meant, any objection to keeping one?"

Everybody laughed. She was much funnier than Mr. Pettit. He told them Clover Lake was an ideal vacation spot and for bringing up children and that we were all a big happy family.

"I guess that covers everything. You'll be hearing from our secretary about your application."

After a little more small talk, the meeting broke up and the Matthews left.

"Nice people," Mr. Pettit said the moment they were gone. Everyone agreed and signed the application. Daddy was the last to leave, having stayed to put the chairs back in place, which is just like him, and found a black patent leather handbag.

"That's hers. Run and give it to them, Jen."

"Run? They'd be miles away by now."

"I doubt it. I doubt if they'd drive all the way up here without stopping to take another look at the house."

I took the shortcut through the knoll and waved the purse as they came along in their car. Mrs. Matthews smiled.

"Did we pass?"

I thought at first she meant, "Did we pass you on the road?" Then I realized she was speaking of the interview.

"Oh, sure. You passed with high marks, both of you."

Mr. Matthews gave me a friendly smile, and Mrs. Matthews said, "We hope to move in right away. Stop in for coffee some afternoon." She spoke as if I were someone her own age.

The velvety caterpillar on her shoulder that I had taken to be a pin moved slightly. I stared in surprise. It was real.

"Yes," she said, as if I had voiced my thoughts. "It's alive. Just matches, doesn't it?"

FOUR

THE MATTHEWS moved in on a Monday. I had sworn I would never step inside that house again, but on Tuesday, there I was.

"Any plans for today?" Mother had asked as she left for work that morning.

"Nothing special."

I take care of the Wilson children almost every afternoon. There's not much else for girls my age to do. We're six miles from the nearest town, and there's no way to get there except by car. Boys, like Shawn Denihee, can hitchhike to the golf course. But I never heard of a girl caddy.

I called for Mark and Debbie Wilson at two and took them to the beach and the playground. At five I returned my charges and wandered back to the house on the fork of the road. Mrs. Matthews had made a real impression on me. It was as if I'd met some legendary character, like Tallulah Bankhead, an actress who once had a home near here. Mother says she was very glamorous, called everybody *Dahling* and drank and swore. I could picture Mrs. Matthews being a younger version of just such a person.

What would she be wearing, I wondered, as I walked past the Hillyer's and then past the neat white house that belongs to the Walshes'? A trailing hostess gown? Gold lamé pajamas? A leopard-skin pants suit?

By day, the Holcombe house (as I still thought of it) was no more spooky than our own. The tower that looked so mysterious at night simply provided a dining room on the ground floor and a bedroom above. As I approached the house, I wondered if I really wanted to go inside—it had been my second home for so many years. And now it would be all different.

As I hesitated, a sound made me look up. There, at the top window, was the face of a small boy—square little chin, short nose, eyes that were somehow old, and an ear-to-ear grin. I raised my hand in greeting, and he disappeared, as if he had been a creature of my imagination, like the leprechaun he resembled.

From the side of the house a throaty voice called, "Come on up. I'm making a garden."

The flagstones of the Holcombes' terrace had been pulled up and stacked to one side. The ground had been spaded. Mrs. Matthews was leaning on a garden fork. She was wearing ragged blue jeans, worn-out sneakers, and a man's shirt. My surprise must have shown in my face, for she laughed. "You don't expect me to wear my best clothes working, do you?"

Embarrassed that she had read my mind, I faltered, "I just stopped by to say hello."

"Hello," she answered, and took off her gardening gloves.

"Oh, don't let me take you from your work, Mrs. Matthews."

"Call me Meeghan."

Her hair was tied back with a shoestring. Her face was shiny. She looked about as glamorous as I did and not much older.

"Did you pull up those flagstones by yourself—Meeghan?" I decided I liked the name after all.

"No. Matt moved them for me last night. I went out and got a few little plants this afternoon. They were just growing wild on that hill over there." She waved toward Burbank Road.

"That's grave myrtle, you know," I told her. The hill belonged to the Methodist churchyard. It was a private cemetery for the Burbanks who owned a lot of land around here years and years ago. They had built the church that used to be there. It's been gone for ages now.

"Thought I saw a couple of tombstones over there." Meeghan watered the plants she had set into the ground

—small, glossy leaves of dark green. In the spring they would have lavender-blue flowers with pretty, square-cut petals.

"I hope nobody minds," she went on. "I'm a scavenger. There's lots more there. Anyway, thinning out is good for plants."

The boy I had seen at the window came out and stood grinning. He had a thatch of yellow hair, bare feet, and a sturdy chest, also bare. "Hi," I said.

"This is Jenny, Pookie. Can you say hello?"

How had she learned my name, I wondered? I couldn't remember telling her. But the child had raised his hand, and his face was serious. "White man speak with forked tongue," he said, and raced off to fling himself into a rope hammock tied between two trees. He swung wildly back and forth until I was afraid he would go sailing out the side, but his mother seemed unconcerned. She took a pack of cigarettes from her pocket, offered it to me, and when I refused, took one herself.

"I'm hot." She brushed a wrist over her forehead. "Let's go in."

As we turned toward the house, I heard a thud. Pookie had fallen. I expected a howl. There was none, though he sat rubbing his knee and wincing.

"Went too high again, didn't you?" Meeghan asked with a fond smile. "You going to be okay? Would you like to have a bandage?" she asked, as if offering a cookie.

He shook his head, scowling, as if he had been caught in a mistake.

"Let's go see if the fudge has hardened," Meeghan suggested and went on.

I followed through the side door into the kitchen. This room, for one, was little changed. The Holcombes' breakfast table and chairs had been replaced by the kind found in old-fashioned ice-cream parlors with curly metal legs. An empty bird cage stood where Mrs. Holcombe had kept her cannisters, on the counter next to the stove. That was all.

Meeghan put a pie tin of fudge on the table and cut it into squares. "Have some," she said, and took a piece herself. It was nice to meet a woman who wasn't worried about calories. I took a piece and bit off a corner.

"Too sweet? Makes me thirsty," Meeghan said, and took two cans of beer from the refrigerator. She opened the tops and pushed one toward me. I took a sip. It tasted awfully sour after the fudge, but I didn't want to seem fussy. I took another sip.

At that moment Pookie came in and said he wanted a drink. He sampled his mother's beer and after a long swallow put the can down. "It's *not* satisfying," he said in answer to some T.V. commercial, I suppose, and went outside again.

Meeghan struck a match on the underside of the table and lit a fresh cigarette. "So what's bothering you?"

Mother had been telling me I was getting a permanent frown, but I had no idea it really showed that much. There seemed no point in saying, "Nothing," so I told her, not very tactfully I suppose, that if it hadn't been for Mr. Pettit and his stupid committee, Diane Holcombe would be in that house right now. And her brother Richie. And Paul Green would be coming to visit.

"How would *you* like it?" I said. "Paul is a very sensitive boy. And very smart. He probably knows the real reason they were turned down. What a bunch of idiots!"

"Who?" Meeghan asked.

"The Membership Committee. The people who interviewed you at the clubhouse."

"They seemed pretty nice to me," she said. "Even the Jolly Green Giant, ho, ho. When I heard we had to be interviewed, I nearly flipped. I thought I'd have to take an aptitude test and give a blood sample. Then all they did was tell us how to find the A&P."

"Sure. The whole thing is a put-on. They just wanted to make sure your grandfather's name wasn't Abraham."

"My grandfather . . . I'll tell you about my grandfather some time." She blew a couple of smoke rings. "So this committee has the power to turn people down. And we passed . . ." A little smile curled the corners of her mouth.

"It's the Committee that decides. I just hate them! Mr. Pettit blows his horn, and the rest of them just follow along. I hate them all!"

If I'd burst out like that at home, Mother would have

said something like, "Hating only harms the hater"; Meeghan nodded in agreement.

"It's good to find somebody you can have a big fat hate on. Healthy. Pours adrenalin into the blood stream. Gives you lots of energy. You've got to let it out, of course."

"I am. I have." Laughing, I told her that I'd cursed them all on devil's beard weed. "But seriously," I said, "I know you're right about letting it out, because at night I dream up all sorts of tortures I'd like for them. And it makes me feel better. Burning in oil. Drowning in quicksand. The Japanese water torture . . ."

Meeghan had picked up a pencil and was doodling on a paper placemat. "What's his name again, the head of the Bund?"

"The chairman? Mr. Pettit. Russell I. Pettit."

She wrote it down. "And the others? Oh, that's right. They'll be on the application."

Meeghan squinted at me through the cigarette smoke like Humphrey Bogart on the Late Show. "You know what would be better than all those tortures? Embarrassment. Ridicule."

It took a minute for me to understand. Then I said, "Oh, yes! You mean . . . what if he suddenly grew a hook nose and couldn't get into certain country clubs! And the others, too. What if they all turned black and weren't wanted in white neighborhoods!"

Meeghan smiled and told me not to get carried away. "Why not dream up something that could really happen? Let's see . . ."

My eyes popped. Something had moved on the stove. Like the stove, it was black and white. I suppose that is why I had not noticed it before. "Is that a *rat?*"

I like mice and hamsters and gerbils and chipmunks. A rat is something else again. This one was black to his waist, or middle, and white from there down, his tail a naked-looking, pinkish-white.

"Don't you like him?" Meeghan reached back and picked it up as if it were a kitten.

To say I didn't like it would have been the understatement of the year. I replied diplomatically that I would like him better if he were white on top and black on the bottom, like a man in a white shirt and dark trousers. "Is that Pookie's?"

"No, he's mine." She cradled him in her arms and gave him a bit of fudge.

"What's his name?" (Not that I cared.)

"Nick." The rat closed its eyes in bliss as she stroked its head with her finger. "I call him Nicky." She stroked his back. "Nicky Pyewackette Peckincrow Greedigutt Elemauzur."

Whether that was his whole name or the Latin name for his particular breed, I did not know. I was considering asking when the door opened and the other Matthews child came in.

"This is Jenny, Niobe. She lives down the road. I hope Jenny will be able to baby-sit for us once in a while."

Niobe narrowed her eyes at me. She was a pale child with a closed-in, secret face, her hair parted in the center and drawn back at both sides like a curtain.

"What's for dinner?"

"What would you like?" her mother asked, still holding the rat.

"Oysters Rockefeller."

"Oysters aren't in season."

I hadn't realized how late it was. "I've got to go. You probably want to start dinner."

"Not really."

I left. As I passed the kitchen windows, she was still sitting as before, patting the rat and crooning, "Nicky, Nicky. Nice old Nick."

FIVE

JUST WHEN I WAS FEELING cheered because of meeting Meeghan, Clover Lake was visited by a plague of caterpillars. They appeared suddenly and were everywhere at once.

They hung by invisible threads from trees, from the eaves, and—it seemed—from the sky itself. Their dirt rained down on the roof and clogged the gutters. The ugly black creatures crawled over everything. It was impossible not to step on them and produce an equally ugly green stain. Daddy swept pailfuls from the driveway; Mother and I brushed them unceasingly from the flagstones and the porch furniture.

Bushes were stripped of leaves, foliage grew thin, flowers were destroyed in a matter of days.

"It's happened in other communities," Mother said. "I guess we couldn't escape forever."

The fact that we weren't the only ones bothered by caterpillars, or tent worms, as some people called them, didn't make things any better, in my opinion.

"This is going to be a great summer," I grumbled. "Diane is lucky to be in Maine."

And then, when my frown was growing deeper than ever, a couple of things happened that put me in a good humor again. Every time I thought of them I had to laugh.

Mr. Pettit drives a big car and has radio controlled doors on his garage. When he's driving home, all he has to do is push a button on a little box in his car, and the garage doors open. They had always worked before, but now, somehow, something went wrong. He drove home one day—and it was pouring rain!—pushed the button, and nothing happened. The doors refused to open. He got soaked trying to get them open and then had to leave his car out all night, because the doors couldn't be forced. And in the morning the car was covered with caterpillars.

Right after that, something else happened. The Pettits have a burglar alarm on their house, which is a two-story affair up on the hill. On this particular night, after they were in bed, Mrs. Pettit heard the cat crying outside. She forgot all about the alarm and went out to get the cat.

Mr. Pettit was asleep. When the alarm went off, he

jumped up and ran around the house looking for the prowler. Mrs. Pettit banged on the door, which had locked behind her and shouted to him to turn off the alarm before it woke the whole neighborhood. It had already automatically alerted the police.

The alarm was howling like a banshee. Mr. Pettit pulled plugs and turned switches but was so flustered he couldn't get it to stop ringing.

The neighbors were wide awake by then and had come out to see what was wrong. The patrol car arrived almost immediately. When Mr. Pettit threw open the front door, there were his neighbors and two policemen gaping at him in his nightshirt!

It was too far away for us to be waked up, but Daddy

heard about it on the train the next day and told us later. When we learned what had happened, I laughed so much I got the hiccups. I was trying to cure them by gulping water without breathing when Mrs. Matthews called to ask if I could baby-sit for them. She wanted me to come at nine.

"At nine?" Mother said. "That's too late for them to get to a nine o'clock movie. I wonder," she mused, "if Mrs. Matthews works at night. I've tried calling her twice—once at ten in the morning and once at noon. The children said she was in bed. I wanted to invite her for coffee."

We had just finished dinner. Daddy went to study French. I went outside and brushed caterpillars from the porch until it was time to leave.

It was growing dark as I started down the road, and the Matthews' house looked spooky, as it always does at night, its odd shape looming like some strange castle against the sky. As I reached the fork, a small figure came trudging up the hill. It was Pookie. This was not the first time I had seen him coming home alone in the dusk from frog-hunting or just poking around one of the piers. He was the most independent child I had ever seen and the most self-sufficient.

"Hi!" I said. "What have you been doing?"

"We been having fun," he said.

"That's nice. Who's 'we'?"

"Me an' a tree."

We went into the house together. The Matthews

were at the kitchen table in old clothes, tall glasses in their hands. Meeghan was barefoot.

"Hi, Jenny," she greeted me, while Mr. Matthews smiled sunnily at all three of us. "Hi, Pook. Catch anything?"

"Wasn't trying." Pookie wandered off.

"Sit down," Mr. Matthews invited.

"I thought you were going out," I said.

"We are," Meeghan said. "It's still early. Sit down and tell us the news."

I started to tell them the story of Mr. Pettit's garage doors and his burglar alarm, but they already knew about it. I suppose Mr. Matthews heard it on the train, too.

"That must have been a rare sight," Meeghan said with a smile. "Old Babbitt in his nightshirt."

"Pettit," I corrected.

"I know. I keep thinking of him as Babbitt. How's everything going?"

"Fine. Except for the caterpillars. They're all over."

"Sorry about that." Meeghan brushed a shred of tobacco from her jeans. "You want something to eat?"

"Me?"

She laughed. "I was talking to Nicky."

The rat was crawling along the counter. She took a dry, brown square from a box and spread it with peanut butter.

"Otherwise he won't eat it," she said. "It's health food. I guess he knows it's good for him, so he avoids it unless I make it appetizing."

Mr. Matthews said they'd better get going. "I'll put the things in the car. See you later, Jenny."

Meeghan put a little cup of water in Nicky's cage.

"What made you want to have a rat for a pet?" I asked.

"My grandmother had a beautiful rat—pure black. You'd have liked my grandmother, Jenny. At seventy-five she could still dance an Irish jig and had flaming red hair. She rinsed it with lime, you know."

Powdered lime, the kind that's made from limestone I wondered, or the fruit? I couldn't ask because Meeghan had gone to the porch with a glass of milk for Pookie.

The rat, I noticed, was licking the peanut butter off his health food. After a minute Meeghan came back and added that her grandmother was known through County Clare for her herbs and medicinal teas.

"County Clare. That's in Ireland, isn't it? Daddy says Gitane is French."

"Grandfather Gitane was a juggling clown with the *Paris Cirque*."

"Did he teach you to juggle?" It wouldn't have surprised me to see Meeghan toss a few pot lids into the air.

"He died when I was three. My father juggled a little, but only to amuse Mother and the other gypsies."

"Gypsies! Your parents were gypsies?"

"Something like that. They wandered. They came

here and got into carnival work before I was born. I traveled around with them. North in summer, South in winter. It wasn't a bad life. I went to school, off and on. Got as far as the seventh grade."

The seventh grade! Maybe that was why she treated me as an equal and wanted me to call her by her first name. But imagine! The child of gypsies! And a French clown for a grandfather! I ached with envy. My own life seemed terribly dull and ordinary. But at least, I thought, I had her for a friend. That was more than Diane had, or anyone I knew.

"Want some potato chips?" Meeghan indicated a bowl on the counter, but I couldn't imagine eating anything in a place where a rat ran free.

"No, thanks. What time are the kids supposed to go to bed?"

"Don't worry about it. They'll go when they're tired."

That made sense, I thought. Meeghan was looking around for her sneakers. She found one in an old school desk they were using for an end table. Pookie spied the other under a wooden porch swing. He crawled underneath to retrieve it and sat up too quickly, knocking his head against the swing.

Crack! He didn't cry this time either, but he did run to his mother for comfort. She gave him a hug. After a moment he whispered a request. "Okay," she answered, and when he had run off happily, she told me, "He wants to take a bath."

"Should I go up?"

"No. He knows where the towels are."

The Matthews left a few minutes later. I watched the taillight go streaking down the hill and went back to the living room. Niobe was watching television.

"Is your brother all right?"

"Why wouldn't he be?"

"I mean, he won't slip in the tub, or anything?"

She looked at me as if I'd suggested he might go down the drain and turned back to her program. After about ten minutes, Pookie came down in his pajamas, damp but rosy-cheeked.

"My head still hurts," he announced, though cheerful.

I didn't know whether he was allowed half an aspirin. "What about a cookie?"

He grinned and ran to the kitchen for one. He shoved it in his mouth, stood on the stair-landing looking at me owlishly, and went up to bed. After a moment his sister went up, too.

I sat looking around the room trying to picture it as it had been when the Holcombes were there. Where their long, gold-colored sofa had stood, was an odd little couch with stiff sides and a metal bottom. After a moment I realized it was the front seat of an old car. The little desk stood at one side of it, a little slatted stool in the shape of an X on the other. A rocking chair and a hassock were in front of the fireplace, and where the Holcombes' leather-topped coffee table had been, was a low table made of a stone slab supported on metal legs.

"I'm a scavenger," Meeghan had said. I could see it

was true. She had decorated the room—if decorated is the right word—with any old things she could find. *Objets trouvés*, Daddy would call them. He always imagines people are burning to know what everything is in French.

Niobe came down the stairs in her pajamas, went to the kitchen, and came back with a plate of cookies and two small bottles of ginger ale.

"Thanks," I said, as she passed them to me. The cookies didn't look gnawed, but I declined them just the same. I drank the ginger ale. Niobe drank hers. Then she took the empty bottles to the kitchen and ran upstairs again. A funny kid.

I wandered around looking for something to read. There were lots of books in the bookcase—books on the theatre, books of poetry, books by authors with long Russian names. Then on a low shelf I saw one that looked like a child's picture book. It was called *A Witch's Garden.* The picture on the cover showed a snake entwined around the roots of a plant. But it was not a book for children.

The illustrations were pen-and-ink drawings of plants. The one in front was of mandrake—"a poisonous plant also known as deadly nightshade. Its forked root is thought by some to resemble the form of a man. Others take it to be the form of the Devil himself."

What an odd book! The drawings throughout were of common plants and flowers, nearly all of them poisonous in either their leaves, their berries, or their stems. Among them were laurel, buttercup, and wisteria. A few plants were beneficial—good for earache or sore eyes, and a few (valerian, mistletoe, and endive) for love potions.

Some had fascinating names: henbane, jimsonweed, oleander. And all of the drawings were nice. The door opened. I jumped and dropped the book on the coffee table. I hadn't heard the car.

The Matthews didn't ask, as people usually do, if the children had given me any trouble. I told them, anyway, that the kids had been good.

There was mud on the knees of Mr. Matthews' jeans. And a twig was caught in Meeghan's hair. "She's determined to have a garden," he told me. But far from complaining, he beamed with admiration. "I guess you want to get home," he said, and took out his wallet.

A shopping list fell to the floor. "Did you get everything you wanted?" I asked, picking it up.

Meeghan looked straight at me and then past me to the coffee table where the little book still lay. "Everything but the deadly nightshade," she said with a smile.

Was she mocking me? I blushed guiltily. I shouldn't have been poking around into their books.

They had brought back some plants, and before I left, they had begun to put them in the garden.

My shadow was black on the road as I left them, and the strange plant names were singing in my head: henbane and hemlock and hemp; wolfbane, jimsonweed, and oleander.

At least three of them had been on that shopping list.

SIX

EVEN AFTER I'D GONE to bed, the names kept repeating themselves in my mind like a chant: hemp and henbane and hemlock; wolfbane, jimsonweed and oleander—suitable plants for a witch's garden.

Suddenly a thought struck me—so delicious that I sat straight up in bed and hugged myself. What if Meeghan were a witch! What a wonderful joke on the membership committee—to have turned down respectable people like the Greens and accepted a witch! It's a wonder I ever got to sleep.

In the morning, I had only to mention the subject of poisonous plants to have it all dispelled with information. Mother gave me an article she had torn from the newspaper some time before. And I found that we had poisonous plants ourselves. Laurel and rhododendron were planted on both sides of the house. We even had poisonous flowers: lily-of-the-valley, larkspur, and iris. It seemed, in fact, that there was hardly anything in the way of ornamental shrubs that didn't contain some harmful chemical or resin.

"You dope!" I told myself, and was thankful Meeghan could not know my suspicions.

I didn't see her for a week or so because I was practicing for the swimming races. There are always three events over the Fourth of July weekend here at Clover Lake. Water sports on Saturday, a cookout on Sunday, and a ball game on Monday—men against the boys.

I hoped the Matthews would come to the races. I'm not very good at most sports, but I'm a good swimmer. There was no sign of them as we passed the house, but their car was in the driveway, so at least they weren't away.

It was funny to be going to the water sports with my parents. Every other year I'd stop for Diane and Richie, and we'd go down together. We three always entered the canoe race together, too.

"Now even their canoe is in Maine!" I sighed as we walked on down the hill.

Mother suggested I enter with Shawn Denihee.

"*Mother!*" Parents never take any notice of time. When Shawn was about ten, he named his boat after me—"Jennifer H." was lettered on the side. And he sent me an enormous valentine. She forgets that was years ago.

"Why? What's the matter with Shawn?" Mother asked.

"Oh, *nothing*. There's *nothing* the matter with *him*. It's the rest of us that don't measure up, now that he goes to Talcott."

"What difference would that make?"

"*Mother!* Kids who go to private schools are all snobs."

"Are they? I went to private school."

Well, in her day things were probably different. A girl who was one of my best friends in the seventh grade went off to Miss So-and-So's school, and the next time I saw her she was talking in this affected voice with a broad *a*. She even said, "I'll have a *hahm*burger." Ick.

At the clubhouse Daddy stopped to say hello to Mr. Walsh, the club president. "The trees aren't too bad down here," he said, looking around. They were mostly evergreens. Apparently the caterpillars don't like them. The oak leaves, however, looked like lace doilies and the maples were threadbare.

"Been up to the Pettits' place?" Mr. Walsh asked. "The trees up there are absolutely bare! Not a leaf."

"Good," I thought. "Serves him right." But looking across the lake I could see that our two willows looked yellowish, as they do in the fall when the leaves are dying.

"Those new people in the Holcombe house are lucky,"

Mr. Walsh went on. "Their trees haven't been touched. Ralph must have had them sprayed before he left."

I suddenly remembered the caterpillar Meeghan had worn on her dress like an ornament that first day and had to smile. Even the caterpillars liked her!

I followed Mother to the beach. People who liked the shade were sitting on the clubhouse porch. Others were finding places on the benches along the boardwalk. A glance told me that Meeghan wasn't among them. I was especially disappointed when one of the women, giggling all the while, told Mother something that had happened to Mrs. Orton. Since Mrs. Orton was on the membership committee, it would have been fun to tell Meeghan about it right then.

Mrs. Orton had been painting the walls of her bathroom. Afterward she began to undress to take a bath and sat down on the hamper to take off her shoes, forgetting she had painted the hamper, also.

"Black paint, too," I could hear myself telling Meeghan. "That's why she's not here. She's having a terrible time getting it off!"

But the races started, and there was still no sign of Meeghan. I entered the intermediate race and came in third. Shawn won, but he's got those long arms and legs. And Jimmy Walsh came in second. As I came out of the water, I saw Mr. Matthews and Pookie. Mr. Matthews had on old clothes—worn jeans and a faded plaid shirt. Pookie had on bathing trunks and a tube.

"Is Meeghan here?" I asked.

"Not yet. She's getting dressed."

Pookie went running to the pier and jumped in. He came up coughing and sputtering, his yellow hair plastered over his face. But almost immediately he was grinning and dog-paddling to the pier, ready to jump in again even though races were going on.

Because there are so many little kids, there were going to be three different tube races. I was bored after the first and swam out to the float. Someone had beat me there, but I didn't realize who it was until I started up the ladder.

"Hi, Jenny!"

I recognized Shawn's voice. His voice isn't that great, but it always gives me a funny feeling in my stomach, which I feel mostly when it's disembodied, like when he's talking over the phone.

"Hi," I answered. But I stayed where I was, *hating* the idea that he might have thought I swam out there because he was there.

"What have you been doing?"

"Nothing." I didn't even look at him. Ever since he started going to Talcott, Shawn is a different person. Not that I've really talked to him—he's never around. But I can tell just by looking at him. His hair is longer, and his clothes have that expensive prep-school look.

I climbed to the top of the ladder, dove in, and swam away. Then, swimming under water, I went back and came up under the float. The water there has a luminous quality, reflecting light from the boards above, and is veined like pale green marble. I love it there. But after a moment I heard a splash and remembered just in time that Shawn and I used to meet under there when we were ten or eleven. I swam away quickly and did the crawl back to the beach.

"Come sit down," Mother said, "they're going to give out the awards."

I stood back of the benches. The women all had on their good sports clothes—slacks or shorts, and I didn't want to get them wet.

A whistle blew. Mr. Walsh was out on the pier with a microphone. Mr. Pettit was beside him, holding the ribbons and trophies. A few had been announced and given out when one of the women said in a low voice, "For heaven's sake! Look what's coming."

Meeghan was crossing the bridge over the dam. She was wearing a long white, lacy dress with flowers in her hair. I dashed over, wishing I could protect her from the criticism of the other women. Her outfit was all wrong for watching water sports here where everything is casual. Meeghan was unperturbed, however, and spun around for me, to show it off. Nor did it bother her to see that the others were dressed as they were.

"We always dress up for the Fourth at home," she said to them. "Don't you do that here?"

They made room for her on the bench.

"Love your dress," Mrs. Parsons said. "It's just precious."

"Thrift shop," Meeghan told her. "It must have belonged to someone's great-grandmother." It was very old-fashioned looking with long sleeves, and Meeghan had looped a necklace of little red and black beads around the high neck.

"That necklace looks darlin' with it," Mrs. Parsons said. "I remember havin' beads like that down home."

With a quick gesture Meeghan took them off and put them over Mrs. Parsons' head. The color matched her red-and-black checked slacks. "Keep them. I have others."

Ribbons were awarded to every child who had entered the tube race—which meant a lot of happy small fry waving them proudly—and Mr. Pettit was beaming like Santa Claus.

Just before the next award, Mr. Pettit took over the mike. "There's a call for Mr. Cohen," he announced, his face mock-serious. "Mr. Sam Cohen. Is Mr. Cohen here?" Then his face broke into a grin to show this was a joke, and he was rewarded with a snicker or two.

Meeghan stood up. "Some of my best friends are

named Cohen," she said in a low voice and walked to the playground. I went with her, and Mother came after us.

"I don't know why he has to say things like that! It's in such poor taste. And the name Sam Cohen! Such a cliché!" Mother added, as if being corny was almost as bad as being prejudiced. "But I do think there was less laughter than when he said it last year."

"Ah, it's an annual witticism." Meeghan had reached the swings.

"There really are a lot of wonderful people here," Mother said, still apologizing.

Meeghan nodded and brushed a caterpillar from the seat of the swing. "Too bad there's such a *blight.*" She gave me a wink and then glanced out to the pier where Mr. Pettit was still standing, the award-giving just over. Her eyes had a hard glitter. They were gray-green, I noticed, with amber flecks. I'd never seen eyes that color.

"How about baby-sitting tonight, Jenny?" she asked.

"Sure."

Pookie was suddenly tugging at his mother's sleeve.

"Hi," she said. "Want a push?"

He shook his head. "I'm going up the slide. Mommy, have I got charisma?"

"Sure you have."

He grinned and ran off to climb *up* the slide like a monkey.

"He's the cutest thing!" Mother said. "Where's your little girl today? Didn't she want to come?"

The swings were low, meant for small children. Meeghan stood on the seat and pumped just enough to make it go a little.

"Niobe's the indoor type. She's probably in the kitchen cooking up some potion or practicing one of her spells."

Mother smiled uncertainly. "There are lots of little girls her age here. Has she met any of them?"

"Only one. Susie Morrow next door. But Mrs. Morrow won't allow Susie to play with Niobe, because Niobe invited her to an esbat. She didn't want her daughter dancing naked on the knoll."

Mother laughed and looked around. "Well, I guess the events are over. Are you coming?" We were heading home.

Meeghan stood there on the swing seat, her two hands on the ropes. "No, I think I'll stay and have a look around."

"See you later," I said, and Mother and I walked on.

Mother was silent for a moment. Then she said, "Charisma! Esbat—whatever that is! Where do they learn such things?"

But then, as if afraid of having sounded too critical, she looked back at Meeghan and said she reminded her of a painting. "You know, that one by Manet of the lady in the swing? You've seen it in that book of Daddy's on the Impressionist painters."

I knew the one she meant. The lady was standing in the same way, holding the ropes and leaning her head against her hand. But the lady in the painting didn't have that hard glitter in her eyes.

Hard, I thought, mischievous and purposeful. Like a grown child planning to do something wicked.

But I was probably imagining all that.

SEVEN

I ARRIVED AT THE MATTHEWS' just before nine. Mr. Matthews was standing by the car, ready to leave. What a nice person he was, I thought, as I did every time I saw him. It was his smile—friendly and sweet and . . . happy, that was it. He always looked happy.

"Hi, Jenny. How are you?" He scanned the deepening sky. "It's a good night, isn't it?" What did he mean? Good for fishing? For stars? Or what?

The front door opened, and his face lit up. Meeghan had come out in a long, loose gown called a caftan, with her hair hanging straight and loose. She looked like some exotic, foreign princess.

But I was disappointed. I'd come early, hoping we might have a visit before they left. To keep her a moment, I told her about Mrs. Orton sitting in the paint: "Imagine. Wet, black paint. Wasn't that wonderful!"

Meeghan smiled modestly as if I'd given her a compliment, and I wondered if she'd misunderstood. "Nothing at all," she said. She tossed her hair, and I caught sight of some odd-looking earrings—a silver face with horns above and wings below.

"The Mexican Devil-God," she said. "We got them in Taxco. See you later." They drove off.

Pookie met me at the door in his pajamas. "I'm getting a skellington."

"A skeleton?" I asked his sister.

"Yes. Of plastic. An educational toy; you put it together."

"He's pretty smart," I said, as Pookie dashed off to the porch swing.

"So am I," she said, matter-of-factly.

"I'll bet you are," I said, and meant it. She was probably smart enough to answer the many questions that had come to my mind since I had met Meeghan, if only I could win her confidence.

"You look like a little gypsy girl," I said, smiling to show I meant it as a compliment. "I love things like gypsies and fortune-telling and esbats." The word wasn't in the dictionary.

Niobe gave me a wary look. She was probably smart enough to know when people were pumping her.

"When I was little," I said, hurrying through the kitchen to avoid the rat, "I loved anything mysterious. I wished I knew the language of the birds or could see things that were invisible. I wished I could see ghosts and witches—not scary ones, of course, good witches who made magic potions and sad little ghosts who were lonely."

A weird cry came from outside, and we both jumped. A quavery *ooooooh! ooooooh!* As the sound was repeated, I smiled at my own foolishness. "That's just an owl, a screech owl." It was a softer sound than a screech, but chilling. "He's probably just calling his mate."

Niobe looked up into my face. "And can you understand what they're saying?"

I laughed. "No. I was just saying what I used to wish."

Pookie had joined us. "I wish I was a magic boy."

"That would be fun, wouldn't it?" I said. "You could turn pebbles into gold, make ugly people beautiful, sick people well."

"And lonely people the most popular ones at school," Niobe said. She was standing close, leaning against me. I had won her over.

"Tell me, Niobe . . ."

But she went swiftly to the stairs. "I'll be in my room." I heard her door close.

Pookie turned on the television. I walked around. In the hall a calendar hung on the wall, the date August first circled in red. Somebody's birthday, I supposed. Or their anniversary.

Passing at the foot of the stairs, I heard Niobe's voice. She must be calling someone from an upstairs telephone. But her voice droned on steadily, without conversational pauses. It sounded more as if she were saying her prayers, but Mr. Matthews had said they didn't go to church.

I tiptoed up the stairs and stood near her door. I could hear the words clearly:

"*Spirits of air, spirits of water,*
Spirits of earth and of fire . . ."

It was a spell! Meeghan had said that afternoon that Niobe might be "practicing one of her spells." But what a funny game for a child to play! Where would she get such an idea? And where would she learn a spell?

The answer was too good to believe. From her mother, if her mother could charm caterpillars to be her ornaments, have a rat for a pet, and plant a witch's garden.

For just a moment I pretended it was possible. Oh, the beautiful justice of it! The Greens turned down and a witch accepted! But of course it was only wishful thinking. I might as well believe I could understand the birds. Or become invisible.

Niobe's door was thrown open. I jumped guiltily, but Niobe didn't seem to mind that I was there. She just wanted to ask a question. "Who are those girls I saw at the beach one day? They were together, three of them.

One had red hair, the other had brown pigtails and one had a green bathing suit."

"Linda Knapp, JoAnne Walsh, and Barbie Hecht. Why?"

"They're coming to play with me tomorrow."

She went back to her room. Just before the door closed, I noticed that Diane's white four-poster bed had been replaced by one with a high, curving headboard and footboard of heavy wood, black as a coffin.

"That's a sleigh bed," Mother told me next morning when I described it. "Is the whole house decorated in Victorian style?"

"I don't know what style you'd call it." I was thinking of the odds and ends in the living room—the sofa made of a car-seat, the table made of a stone slab. "There's a funny lamp in the dining room. A red and green glass shade that hangs down on a chain."

"A Tiffany shade of leaded glass!"

"It doesn't look like Tiffany's to *me*. It says Coca-Cola on it."

Mother didn't find that odd in the least. She said those old shades were very popular right now and that people often asked for them at the shop. Especially the Coca-Cola ones.

It was raining. The cookout would have to be postponed. I stood at the window, wondering what to do. Three little girls in raincoats were walking to the Matthews' house—Linda, JoAnne, and Barbie. I remembered Niobe's satisfied smile when she said they were coming. Maybe because Mrs. Morrow, who lived right next door to the Matthews', wouldn't let Susie play with Niobe. She'd be sure to see them going to the house. I was about to remark on this to Mother, when the telephone rang. I answered it, although all my friends from school are away at camp or at the seashore.

"Is your father home, dear?" It was Mrs. Pettit, sounding bright and cheery as usual. "Don't bother calling him. I'll give you the message. I'm calling for Mr. Pettit." Her laughter tinkled over the wire. "I'm his Girl Friday."

I wrote it down. Membership meeting. One o'clock today. To meet the people who wanted to buy the Grant house.

"We're sorry to make it on a holiday," Mrs. Pettit said. "But we usually have these meetings on Sundays, when people are home from work, you know. And Mr. Grant asked us to put this one through quickly, if we could. His company is transferring him to Baltimore, and he has to sell his house right away. I'll stop by with the application."

I read the application myself when she dropped it off. *Mr. and Mrs. Thurlow Brook. Self-employed. Children's names, Sally, Edward, Gregory.* I put it on the hall table where we always leave the mail and messages and stood dreaming. What if Sally were just my age, and her brothers, thirteen and fourteen . . .

By noon the rain had almost let up. Birds were singing noisily, and my own spirits rose. I asked Daddy if I could go to the clubhouse with him. It was sprinkling a little. Daddy held his umbrella over both of us and read the application as we walked along.

"Hm. Sound like an interesting family. Mr. Pettit tells me Mr. Brook is a historian. Writes books on ancient Troy and Persia and has done translations of Russian poetry."

In that case, I thought, the boys would probably be Brains, like Paul Green. That would be okay with me. Or they could be athletes. As long as they and their sister were somewhere near my age and not in the Playpen Set.

"They ought to make them tell their children's ages on those applications."

Daddy didn't agree. "They ask too many questions as it is. 'Father's name . . . Mother's name . . . Wife's maiden name.' It's none of our business whether they're Christians or Hottentots."

I remembered what Mrs. Orton had said about minorities and property values.

"Daddy, would you vote for minorities moving here even if it meant getting less money for the house if you sold it?"

Daddy stopped by the bulletin board to knock a few caterpillars to the ground and step on them. The ink had run on a notice that said the annual cookout and baseball game would be postponed due to the rain.

"I like money as much as anybody, Jenny," Daddy

said, "but what's money for? To make us happy, isn't it? I couldn't feel happy if I'd said to somebody, 'You're not good enough to live here.' "

The rain suddenly came down harder. We ran to the clubhouse. The beach was deserted, of course. The sand was pitted with little holes, the benches puddled, the sky gray. I helped Daddy move the chairs in a circle, and the others arrived, all but Mrs. Parsons who wasn't feeling well. Mr. Pettit was not his usual jolly self, but complaining about petty vandalism. He'd noticed that a photograph of club officers was missing from the card room.

"We've got to keep the kids out of here," he said. "Give them an inch and they . . ."

He was interrupted by the arrival of the Brooks. Oh, *dear*, I thought, now we'll *never* know the end of that *fascinating* sentence. "Give them an inch and they'll . . . what?" Such corn.

The Brooks were middle-aged. Mr. Brook had a gray beard and Mrs. Brook wore glasses. They looked interesting, though. We've never had an author at the lake, and Mrs. Brook looked as smart as her husband. I didn't stay, however. Not after Mr. Pettit's crack about kids in the clubhouse. Daddy would tell me about the children's ages.

"They're of college age," he said when he came home. "That is, the boys are in college. The daughter's married. But it doesn't matter. The sale is off."

"You mean they were turned down?"

"They turned *us* down."

"They turned the *club* down?" Mother asked. "Why?"

"Mrs. Brook does social work. She didn't like the idea of people being 'screened,' as she put it. She said she would feel hypocritical living in such a place. I can't say I blame her. It's too bad. They're extremely nice people, but this may be just what we need. Shake people up a bit."

"I'll bet everyone on the committee was surprised," Mother said.

Daddy nodded. "Sally Lou wasn't there, but Bill Hillyer and Sylvia Orton were speechless, and as for Russell, I thought he'd pop. His mouth fell open and his face got red. He's probably telling people that the Brooks are Communists."

"I can imagine it," Mother said.

"Poor Russell," Daddy went on, "he's got a bad case of poison ivy, and that was bothering him, too. Where are you going, Jenny?"

I called from the doorway that I'd be right back. I couldn't wait to tell Meeghan the news. It was such a good joke on the committee.

Mr. Matthews and Niobe were in the kitchen. Pots and bowls stood everywhere on stove and counters. They were making supper.

"Meeghan's been working all afternoon," he explained.

She was on the car-seat sofa reading a book. Pookie was nearby playing on the floor with a narrow picture frame. I told Meeghan about the Brooks.

"Isn't that a switch? *They* disapproved of the *club*. It's a real kick in the stomach, isn't it? And guess what else? Mr. Pettit has poison ivy."

Meeghan put down her book. "Yes, but the best part is how he got it. Did you hear?"

"Weeding, I think Daddy said."

Meeghan lifted her long hair from her neck and gave me a lazy smile. "He got it clearing the wandering Jew out of his pachysandra."

Wandering Jew. That trailing weed with little blue flowers. "No fooling?" I burst out laughing. "Oh, but Meeghan. That's perfect."

"Thanks," she said.

Her answers are sometimes hard to figure.

EIGHT

On Monday it rained again. The sky was so dark Mother had the light on in the kitchen as she mixed a cake. She hated cooking, but she didn't mind baking. I stood at the window, watching the rain splatter down. I could only hope that the caterpillars were drowning.

"There they go again," Mother said, glancing toward the road. "Don't they look cute in their raincoats? I wonder where they're headed in this rain?"

"They're going to play with Niobe." It was the same three girls. They were walking toward the Matthews'.

"Oh, good!" Mother said, "I'm glad to see Niobe's made friends."

On Saturday afternoon Meeghan had told us that

Niobe hadn't met anyone but Susie Morrow. That night Niobe had told me these three were coming to play with her—and they had. And now they were going there again. Had Niobe's "spell" really worked to summon them? Or had she simply telephoned and invited them the next morning?

Come to think of it, Meeghan seemed to know about things before I told her. She had known about Mrs. Orton sitting in paint and about Mr. Pettit's burglar alarm and about his poison ivy. It was creepy.

I thought of confiding in Mother, but hesitated for fear she might not allow me to go to the Matthews'. Daddy was at the table balancing the check book. The percolator was burping on the stove. After a moment Daddy gathered up his papers and left the room, and I questioned Mother, tip-toeing around the subject.

"Mother, is there such a thing as mind-reading and being able to tell the future?"

Mother put her cake in the oven and poured a cup of coffee. "I think there must be something of the sort. When I was at boarding school, our housemother used to play piano, and we girls would stand around and sing. One night she told us she knew a woman who had second sight, as she called it. She didn't tell fortunes or anything. Not for money, anyway. It was a 'gift,' she said, like having perfect pitch.

"Well, this woman told our housemother, Mrs. MacCartan, that she saw her with a lot of children. Mrs. MacCartan said, 'You're wrong. I've just lost my husband, and I know I will never marry again.' But the woman insisted, 'Yes, I see you at a piano and girls standing all around.' And there we were."

I listened dreamily, picturing myself one of those girls. I always liked hearing Mother's boarding school stories. I had forgotten why I had asked the question.

"Why? Who's been reading your mind?"

"No one. It's just that sometimes Mrs. Matthews seems to know what I'm thinking."

Mother laughed. "You have a very mobile face, Jenny. I don't think it would be hard to tell what you're thinking at times. But I know what you mean. She seems to answer questions before you've finished asking them."

"I didn't know you knew her," I said, surprised.

"She was walking by last week. It was my day off, and I asked her in. You were at the beach. You know what I think? I think she's just awfully bright and quick. She was probably at the head of her class in college, on the dean's list and everything."

I remembered what Meeghan had told me about her schooling but thought it best not to mention it.

"She's interested in all sorts of things," Mother said. "Politics and playwrights and serious novelists. You should hear her rattle off those difficult names: Nabakov, Solzhenitsyn, Kazantzakis, as if she were saying her ABC's! I enjoyed talking to her."

Mother rinsed her cup and took an experimental peek in the oven. I got a whiff of cake baking, all lemony and fragrant. "Mrs. Matthews is bright all right," Mother said. "But she has a rather cryptic way of talking. None of the rest of us can figure what she means most of the time. Did she mention what college she went to? Maybe it was Duke University where they do experiments with ESP."

"ESP? What's that?"

"Extra-sensory perception. You don't hear so much about that nowadays. There's such a tremendous boom in mysticism, astrology, and witchcraft."

"Witchcraft!"

"Yes, it's the big thing, now. I think it all started with that book, *Rosemary's Baby*. I read the book, and then Mary Holcombe and I saw the movie. Daddy wouldn't go, of course. He said 'Rubbish.' It was about a group of witches in New York—both men and women witches who did awful things and made them seem accidental—heart attacks, suicide . . ." Mother gave a little shudder.

"Why didn't you take us—Diane and me? We'd have liked it."

"No. It was really quite upsetting, in view of the fact that there are supposed to be witches practicing in Connecticut and Westchester and everywhere."

"Honestly, Mother? Real witches?"

"Calm down, Jenny. I didn't say they were *real*. I should certainly hate to think there were people like that—so called Satanists. They worship the devil. Which means, I suppose, that they like doing evil for its own sake. Then there are supposed to be good witches, who say they would never use their powers to harm anyone except in punishment for wrong doing."

"They *say* . . . ? You mean they come right out and *admit* . . . ?"

"Admit being witches? Why not? It's a kind of religion to them. They're not ashamed of it. They consider themselves real do-gooders. Like Sybil Leek. She says she's a hereditary witch—you know, that it came down to her through her grandmother or great-grandmother. If you're not lucky enough to have witch's blood in your veins," Mother said with a smile, "then you have to go and take a course somewhere."

"A course! You mean you can go study witchcraft the way you'd study to be a nurse or something?"

"Apparently. According to this article I once read in the *New York Times*. They had an interview with some witches . . ."

"The *New York Times!*"

"Yes, it was really fun. Sybil Leek was one of them. She's world famous. Then I remember an article in *Life* magazine some time ago. That was about witches on the West Coast. Jenny, if you don't stop jumping around, my cake is going to fall. The article in *Life* was more sensational than the one in the *Times*. It showed photographs of these people in their homes. A man, for instance, tall and dark with a beard, who wore a cloak and went in for spooky gadgets like having a lighted skull for a lamp. That seemed awfully faky. But he apparently has quite a following out there."

I was amazed. The idea of witches being interviewed and photographed by respectable newspapers and magazines!

"And one, a woman," Mother went on, "was quite young and attractive. So were her children. She had a rat for a familiar. A black and white one."

I looked up quickly. Was Mother teasing me? Did she know about Meeghan's rat? But apparently not, for Mother's face was serious. My heart began beating fast.

Despite certain evidence, I hadn't allowed myself to dare believe anything so crazy as that Meeghan was really a witch. And here was my own Mother and *Life* magazine and the *New York Times* all thrown at me like an icy shower!

"Mother, could we go to the library?"

Our library keeps a file of old magazines. I had to get hold of that copy of *Life*. I couldn't wait to see the photograph of the young witch with the black and white rat.

But I *had* to wait. It was a holiday. The library was closed. Not that I needed proof. Things had started to happen the moment Meeghan arrived. And to people *I* had selected! She had taken my enemies for her own and played tricks on them. No wonder she had said "Nothing at all," when I told her about Mrs. Orton. She meant, "That was nothing." She was being modest. No wonder she had said "Thanks," when I said Mr. Pettit's poison ivy was perfect! And what about the plague of caterpillars?

I went out and whirled around on the porch unable to sit still. How did I get so lucky? Imagine having a witch for a friend! Point out an enemy and—pft!—something funny happened to him. It was too good to be true. I hadn't really believed in witches. But if the *New York Times* said so . . .

Mother took the cake out of the oven, and the kitchen was filled with the fragrant smell of lemon.

"Mmm. I can't wait till dinner time."

"This isn't for us. It's for the Parsons'. Poor Sally Lou! It's bad enough having it rain and the kids cooped up in the house, but she's got—I don't know, something or other."

I almost laughed aloud. Another committee member bites the dust, I said to myself. "What's she got? Poison sumac from pulling *black*berry vines out of her garden?" I thought this so clever that I repeated it with an explanation. "You know: like Mr. Pettit getting poison ivy pulling wandering *Jew* from his pachysandra?"

Mother gave me a reproving look. "There's nothing funny about it, Jenny. Sally Lou is very sick."

"You mean sick in bed?"

"As a matter of fact, she's been violently ill. Thank goodness the rain has stopped. I think I'll walk up with this and see if she needs help."

"I'll take it," I said. My feeling of elation had subsided.

Mrs. Hecht, the Parsons' next door neighbor was there, helping out, trying to cook and keep the children quiet. Mrs. Parsons was in bed. I offered to stay and mind the children a while. The doctor was expected.

He came while I was there. I heard Mrs. Hecht tell him how Mrs. Parsons had been vomiting. Mrs. Parsons tried to joke about the mess her room was in. She sounded weak, but she's not the type to feel sorry for herself.

After a while the doctor came out to the kitchen and told Mrs. Hecht (while he washed his hands at the sink) that Mrs. Parsons had ingested poison of some kind. But he was puzzled. She hadn't eaten anything she hadn't given the rest of the family, and *they* were all fine. He had noticed that Mrs. Parsons bit her nails and had wondered about her nail polish. But it was a well-known brand and harmless. He would have to make tests.

As he was leaving, the doctor noticed a necklace on the hall table and went back to ask Mrs. Parsons if she ever bit on the beads.

"*You* try takin' care of this house and these kids," she retorted with a laugh, "and *you'd* chew more than beads!" Mrs. Parsons is always spirited, even when she's sick.

The necklace was the one Meeghan had given her at the beach, made of little red and black beads. The doctor said they were precatory beans and told Mrs. Parsons to throw them out. The beans, found in tropical countries, were made into necklaces and sold widely, but they were poisonous.

Mrs. Hecht sent the children out to play. She said I might as well go home. I went to the bedroom door to tell Mrs. Parsons I hoped she'd feel better.

"Thanks a million," she said. "I never would have got any rest with those little monsters racing around. Tell your mother thanks for the cake, hear?"

"O.K."

"Everyone's been just wonderful. Ginny Walsh took my laundry to do in her washer, and Kay Wilson sent over a meat loaf."

Kindness is nothing new at Clover Lake, I thought as I left. If anybody's in trouble, if they have an accident or a fire or anything, everybody helps in one way or another. It's a great place to live. You just have to have the right color skin and the right ancestors.

The tree trunks were dark amidst the thin foliage. It looked like spring, when the leaves are just coming. Couldn't it be a coincidence that the caterpillar plague had come when it had—just after I had told Meeghan my complaints about the committee? Lots of other places had caterpillars, I told myself.

I thought of stopping in at the Matthews' to tell Meeghan—as a kind of test—about Mrs. Parsons getting sick on those beads. Would she say, "Nothing to it," or something like that?

Now, wait a minute, I said. Be fair. Meeghan may have given her those beads, but she didn't tell her to *chew* them. She didn't make Mr. Pettit pull up those weeds. Or Mrs. Orton sit in that paint! People got into wet paint all the time. That's why they have printed signs: WET PAINT.

I *would* go in, I decided. They owed me money, anyway. Mr. Matthews hadn't had the right change the last time I sat for them, the time I heard Niobe chanting. I stood on the road looking toward their house. The geraniums in the window boxes shone gaily through the gloom. This was the cheerful side of the house. To the left was the garden. It started there on the upper road and slanted downward, going half way down to the lower road. The rest was grass.

Niobe came to the door when I knocked. She was the only one home, but she told me they had left my baby-sitting money. "It's there, on the coffee table."

As I picked up the envelope with my name on it, I noticed for the first time that there was lettering cut into the table-top.

R.I.P.
Here lie the Earthly Remains of
Hester P. Burbank
Beloved Wife of Ezra Burbank
Feb. 13, 1803 — Nov. 2, 1864

It was a tombstone. "It's just another 'Found Object,' " I told myself, "like the car-seat sofa and the Coca-Cola lamp shade." But my arms were all goose pimples.

NINE

On television, librarians are usually old and stodgy. Real librarians aren't like that. At least ours aren't. They're nice looking and wear smart clothes.

But they're almost too helpful. I mean, if you're looking for something, they run all over the place finding reference material until you feel you ought to be doing something great and not just satisfying your curiosity.

"I know which one you mean," Mrs. Dickson, our librarian said, when I spoke of the *Life* magazine. "I'll see if it's in. Look in section H 521, in the meantime. We have quite a few books on witchcraft, but there's so much interest in the subject we have a hard time keeping them on the shelf."

The grown-ups were really shaking me up, taking such a matter-of-fact attitude about something I'd been afraid even to mention. There were a lot of books in section H 521, but most of them were on the witch trials in Salem. Others were on Edgar Cayce, on astrology and related subjects. I selected three with promising titles: *The Devils of Loudon*, *Witchcraft in Our Time*, and *Black Magic and White*.

When I went to check them out, Mrs. Dickson was poring over a thick volume called *Books in Print*, looking for other titles for me.

"That was quick," she said, taking my books. "If you're interested in fiction about witches, I can give you a list."

"Maybe later," I said, eager to get on with it. "Did you find the magazine?"

She held it up. "You're in luck. Someone just returned it. Try to return it in a week, will you? It's very popular."

I said I would look at it right there and took it to one of the reading tables. I was shaking a little as I turned the pages, half-hoping, half-afraid to find Meeghan looking back at me from a glossy photograph. I found the article. The woman said to be a witch did have a black and white rat, black on top, white on the bottom, just like Nicky. But she wasn't Meeghan. Her hair was dark and her features completely different. I read the whole article and returned the magazine to the desk.

"Have a nice day," Mrs. Dickson called as I left. She

apparently saw nothing odd in my choice of books.

"Thanks. You, too."

Bees hummed over the pink and purple rhododendrons planted outside the library. Sun shone through the trees, dappling the sidewalk with moving patterns. It was hard to believe in witches on such a bright summer day.

Mother, at the wheel of the car, waved to me to hurry. She was on her lunch hour and had to get back to the shop. "Find what you wanted?"

"Mmm." I kept the books face down. I hadn't told Mother why I wanted to go to the library. I didn't want to talk about witchcraft any more. I wanted to find out about it for myself.

I felt mixed up inside, not knowing what to believe, not knowing what I wanted to be true. But if the woman in *Life* magazine—a nice-looking, normal-looking woman with two children—could be a witch, then Meeghan could be one.

At Clover Lake Mother drew up at the row of mailboxes, and while I was yanking out all the junk mail that stuffs our box, Meeghan came along in her car. She drew up beside Mother and asked with a smile, "Wanta drag?"

Mother asked, "What?" Meeghan laughed and drove on.

"What did she mean? Drag *what?*"

"She was joking, Mother. She meant drag race."

"Oh."

Mother slowed down as we passed the Matthews' place. The garden was enclosed with castor bean vine, which had grown up in just a few weeks, like Jack's beanstalk. Pookie was climbing a knotted rope that hung from one of the trees.

"Isn't he fantastic!" Mother said. "He really looks more like an elf than a human child. I keep feeling that if I lift up that hair I'll find pointed ears."

It was exactly my opinion, but I felt a twinge of disappointment that his elfin quality should be recognized by others. I had considered it my own discovery.

We hurried on home. Mother had a cottage cheese salad, took an apple with her, and drove off. I ate a sandwich and carried my books and some cookies to the smaller of our two willows and climbed up a warty limb to a flat place where I like to read.

The Devils of Loudon proved to be about witch trials in France long, long ago. *Witchcraft in Our Time* was surprising in that it was as factual as a textbook. It stated that there were four hundred or more witches' covens in the United States. They held monthly meetings called *esbats*, it said (so that's what it meant!), and eight yearly festivals called *Sabbats*. The most important of these was held on Lammas, which was—the date jumped out at me from the page!—August 1st.

Witches, I read, liked to live at a place "where two roads meet, for this is considered lucky." Whenever possible they held their meetings near the water, for they considered water magic. They met at night to perform their rites and ceremonies and were greatly interested in night skies for "their best work is done by the rise of the moon." Witches' children might themselves be witches, or not. The word *warlock* was passé and was no longer used to designate a male witch by those in the Craft, who used the word *witch* for both sexes. Courses in witchcraft were now being offered in several colleges and universities. These dry statements made witches sound as real as grocers or carpenters.

It was time to call for the Wilson kids. I stopped for them and went to the beach, taking a book along. The Wilson kids were a little afraid of the water. I always had to coax them in. They preferred digging in the sand and playing at the water's edge. Today I let them do that and sat nearby to read.

From the book called *Black Magic and White* I learned that there were two kinds of witches. "White" witches referred to witchcraft as "the Old Religion." They worshiped the Great Spirit, busied themselves brewing herbs for healing, making unguents for warding off pain, and mixing love potions.

These witches were scorned by their more powerful sisters, the "black" witches, who worshiped Satan and did his bidding. These performed black magic, used herbs and plants that were toxic, and brought pain or death to a victim by performing rites over his photograph or his name written in longhand.

"The turning point in a witch's career comes early," I read. "While still a novice, she must choose for good or evil. At this moment her choice may be influenced by various things: The phases of the moon, the position of the stars, by another witch, or even by an outsider."

Even an outsider. I felt shivery, although the sun was showering diamonds on the bright blue water and sending blinding reflections from the steel ramp of the slide.

I didn't want to read any more, but my eyes went back to the book the way your tongue will keep seeking out a tooth that hurts if touched.

Witches usually kept cats as pets or "familiars," but often kept crows, toads, or other creatures. Common names for these familiars were Pyewacket, Pecke-in-the-Crowe, Elemausar, and Grizzled Greedigutt. Nick, Old Nick, Old Scratch were names for the Devil. Puki, an old Norse word, also meant the Devil. Spelled various ways—Puke, Puck, Pukki—it could mean a mischievous sprite (as Puck, in Shakespeare's *A Midsummer Night's Dream*), a goblin, or an elf.

And finally, witches never cry.

TEN

FOR THE NEXT FEW DAYS I avoided the Matthews and tried not to think about Meeghan. But at almost any time of day or night, arguments would rage in my mind.

Meeghan was a witch, and perhaps a wicked one. She had chosen a house on a fork "where two roads meet." It was near the water, and water was magic. There were poisonous plants in her garden. She had a rat for a pet or "familiar" who was named for the Devil. Niobe had summoned three girls with a witch's chant. And Pookie never cried.

Then I'd remind myself that our good friends, the Holcombes, had lived on a fork of the road near the water. There were poisonous plants around our own house and around the library. True, Meeghan had a book called *A Witch's Garden*, but hadn't my mother kept an article on the same subject? As for the rat, hadn't I, myself, kept a bat for a week a few years ago? Didn't my grandmother have a canary called Nicky? Niobe might have found that chant in a book borrowed from the library. Hadn't Mrs. Dickson said that such books were so popular she could hardly keep them on the shelf? Niobe could have been playing *Magic Spell.* And why shouldn't the little girls come to play with her? Their mothers had probably prompted them, saying, "Go play with that new little girl; she hasn't any friends." And how did I know that Pookie *never* cried?

To get rid of these pesky arguments I did things I would not have done otherwise: straightened my bureau drawers with my record player blasting; let down the hems of two dresses; and wrote to Diane, although I'd had nothing but a postcard from her (Had lobster for dinner last night—yummy.) since she'd been gone.

I didn't mention Meeghan in my letter, for that would have taken pages and pages, and besides I wasn't sure as yet what Meeghan really was. So I wrote:

Dear Di:
What are you doing besides eating lobster? How's the swimming? Are there any good kids up there? Have you met any nice boys? Are you ever coming down here for a visit? How's Richie? Have you heard from Paul?

It was like a quiz, all questions, but I mailed it anyway with just a p.s. to say that I'd miss her this weekend when we were going to have the postponed cookout and ball game.

The cookout is one of the times I'm glad I'm not a grownup. (The other is when we go to a Howard Johnson's and I have a double scoop of two terrific flavors and my parents order just cups of coffee. I hope I never get that old!)

The kids eat at six. We have hot dogs or hamburgers cooked over charcoal. The grownups have to wait till eight, and then they get shish-kebabs: hunks of lamb, whole onions, and green pepper. I hate green pepper, and who'd want to eat all those onions? Yechh!

Well, as Daddy says, "*Chacun a son gout*," which is the French equivalent of, "It's *your* stomach." The hamburgers were great.

The day of the game was warm and sunny and cloudless. And what with the bright weather and so much going on, I forgot about witchcraft. Even when I saw the Matthews. Meeghan was wearing a long, patchwork skirt and had her hair tied up with colored yarn. She looked beautiful. Mr. Matthews had on the usual old faded jeans and a plaid shirt and hadn't shaved. That's the way he always looks weekends. During the week he looks like any commuter going to work on Madison Avenue.

I wore my cheerleader's outfit and led a cheer for the

boys. Daddy catches for the men's team, but we kids always stick together.

At the start of the third inning, Mr. Hillyer was up at bat. Shawn was on the pitcher's mound.

"Come on, Dads!" Mr. Pettit shouted. "Don't let the youngsters beat you. Youth isn't everything." Turning around to the benches, he said to the ladies, "Youth is such a wonderful thing, it's a shame to waste it on the young, ha ha." (Brand new joke, *circa* 1936.)

Shawn wound up. The ball shot over the plate. Mr. Hillyer suddenly dropped his bat and doubled up. Everyone thought he'd been hit by the ball.

"Keep back. Give him air!" Mr. Pettit ordered.

Mr. Hillyer raised his head. "Cramps," he said, and collapsed. Mr. Walsh and Mr. Wilson carried him from the field. Daddy drove him home. A little later the Hillyers' car went by. Mrs. Hillyer was taking him to the doctor.

Then other men came back, and the game went on. The boys' team won, but it wasn't much of a victory. Mr. Hillyer is the star of the men's team. There wasn't much cheering. People went home. Mr. Walsh took the boys' team to a pizza place. I walked to the beach.

Mother and Daddy had gone home. The Matthews had driven off in their car with their children. I had a feeling of let-down, the way you feel when you've been looking forward to a party for a long time, and it's over. The way you feel on Christmas afternoon.

I swam to the float. With the boys gone off for pizza

and the little kids going home for supper, the lake was practically deserted. The life guard goes off duty at five. I had always wanted to try swimming home from the club. Today, I decided, would be the day.

I swam underwater a while, seeing little specks of weed and algae rise slowly to the surface. I did the crawl till I was tired, turned on my back and floated. I did the backstroke a while and, by alternating, made it all the way home.

I climbed over the fallen stones, stretched out on the lawn to rest, and then walked triumphantly to the house. Instead of congratulating me on my feat, Mother blew up.

"Your lips are blue. Get out of that wet suit this minute. The idea of swimming all that distance with no one around!" She followed me around, growing more excited as ideas of what might have happened came to mind.

"You might have been hurt!" There are snapping turtles in the lake, but they've never bothered anyone. So far. "You might have had a cramp . . ."

"Oh, Mother! People only get cramps in cold water. Clover Lake isn't . . ."

"You can get cramps from eating. Look at Mr. Hillyer. What did they say?" This last question was addressed to Daddy who had been on the telephone.

"They say it was food poisoning of some kind. They're not sure how he got it."

I had on my bathrobe, but I began to feel shaky. My

fingers were all shriveled. I didn't feel like eating, although normally a long swim would leave me ravenous.

"You know better than to swim that far," Mother scolded, when I refused my dinner. "You should have someone go along in a boat, if you want to try something like that. Or at least tow an inner tube along. When I think of what could have happened!"

"She's home safe, Amy," Daddy said. "Don't let your imagination run away with you. Go up to bed if you like, Jenny. I'll bring you a tray later."

I wasn't cold, and it wasn't the swim. What was troubling me was the word "poisoning." Mr. Hillyer was on the Membership Committee. An idea I did not want to admit kept pushing at the door of my mind.

"I'm *not* responsible," I insisted. "It's Meeghan's fault." But was it? I had complained to Meeghan about the committee. I remembered what the book on black magic had said about novice witches: that early in their careers, when they were first learning their craft, they could be influenced toward good or evil by the moon, the stars, another witch, *or an outsider*.

I remembered that there were many charms and chants, many ways of bringing one's wishes to pass. What if I had summoned Meeghan, somehow, by wishing on the devil's beard weed?

Rubbish, I said. You *know* there's nothing to those old stories. Devil's beard can't bring evil any more than four-leaf clovers can really bring good luck. And you

know there's no such person as the Devil. It's just an idea. A symbol.

Daddy came in a little later to say Mother was making a light supper for me. I decided to question him discreetly. Since he reads the encyclopedia the way other people read their mail, you can ask him anything.

"Daddy is there such a thing as evil influence, like putting the evil eye on someone?"

"Some people believe in mental influences," Daddy said, perching on the foot of my bed. "They believe there is an indefinable spiritual, or psychic quality, an influence from one mind to another, but there is no way at present to prove or disprove it."

He moved back more comfortably and went on, "Whether the thought of one person can influence or act upon another is something for which there is *some* evidence, as in hypnotism and healing. But a person must be willing to be hypnotized and cooperate to a certain extent; and in healing, of course, a person is eager to be affected, and therefore his own thinking may largely account for the results, if any."

He wasn't through. That's one trouble with asking him.

"However," he concluded, "I am completely skeptical about such things myself."

In other words, negative. I felt better. Daddy had such a logical mind. When Mother came in with my tray, I finished everything on it. Mother said my eyes were brighter.

"I believe you were hungry and didn't know it! Get a good rest and plan something nice for tomorrow. Mrs. Wilson called to say she won't need you. She's taking the children to the circus. Mrs. Morrow was going, too, and taking Susie. But her water pipes have broken, and her place is in a mess! What a time for it to happen! Her in-laws are on their way from New Jersey for a visit."

"What made that happen?"

"Who knows? I was just saying to Daddy, I don't even want to answer the phone any more. Every time it rings, it's just somebody reporting some kind of trouble."

I relaxed. Trouble came to everyone, not just people

on the Membership Committee. Mrs. Morrow wasn't on the committee. And then I thought of something. Mrs. Morrow was Meeghan's next-door neighbor, and she wouldn't let Susie play with Niobe. Was this another of Meeghan's tricks? If so, it let me off the hook. I'd never wished Mrs. Morrow any harm. But it was another proof of Meeghan's power. It was scary.

"Mother, Mr. Hillyer's going to be all right, isn't he?"

"Oh, yes!" Mother said brightly. "I meant to tell you. He's coming home tomorrow. And they found out what caused it. The strangest thing! The poison came from a stick."

"A *stick!*"

"Yes. The one his shish-kebab was cooked on. Luckily no one else got the same kind. The poison got into the meat."

I felt a prickling along the back of my neck. "Where did it come from, that stick?"

Mother said the supper chairman had sent children around collecting. They had picked up a few here and there from different places around the community. "I don't know who around here has oleander."

I knew.

It was one of a group of plants whose names had stuck in my mind: "Hemp and henbane and hemlock; wolfbane, jimsonweed and oleander. Suitable plants for a witch's garden."

It grew dark, and I was still awake. The sky turned

navy blue. The big maple outside my window tapped against the pane. Normally that tree was full of leaves, but this was not a normal summer. A yellow moon slid in a stealthy way through the bare black branches.

It was mid-July, but it felt like Hallowe'en.

ELEVEN

IF YOU LIVE ON A LAKE, you don't need to look at the sky to tell what kind of day it is. You can tell by the water. If there's a mist rising, the air is cooler than the water. Ripples from the north mean it will be fair but colder. Ripples from the east usually mean rain. And if there are little dimples all over the surface, it's raining already.

That morning the lake was a mirror, mostly dark green in color from surrounding trees and lawns. I went downstairs in my pajamas. Daddy had gone to play tennis before his tutoring class. Mother was drinking coffee standing up, ready to go to work. It was nine-thirty; the shop opens at ten.

"Have a good rest?" My breakfast was laid out.

"What are you going to do today?"

"Haven't decided."

"No long-distance swimming," Mother said firmly.

"I wasn't tired at all. I was worried about Mr. Hillyer. Honestly."

"We all were. But he's going to be fine. He's coming home today." At the door Mother turned concernedly. "I *don't* want you to stay in a brood. There's nothing for you to be worried about. I mean it, now. Have fun. Enjoy yourself."

I ate some cereal and cleaned up the kitchen. I didn't want to have fun. I didn't feel like enjoying myself. How could I—knowing what I did about the poisoned shishkebab and the broken water pipes and everything else?

It had all been spoiled, I thought, as I made my bed. It *could* have been such fun, knowing a witch, having her do all sorts of things with her power. Well, as Mrs. Milton, our social studies teacher once wrote on the blackboard: "Power corrupts, and absolute power corrupts absolutely." Maybe it wasn't possible to have power and just use it for fun.

When I was dressed, I filled a pail with water and carried it to the Morrows' house. They have one of the prettiest places here. It usually looks neat as a Christmas package, soft green with white trim. Today a deep trench had been dug in front. There were muddy hoses, wheel barrows, shovels, and a huge pile of dirt. Two workmen in brown-stained white overalls were busy at one end of the trench.

Mrs. Morrow came to the door. "Oh, thank you, Jenny. We can use some more water. Isn't this place a mess? They're still trying to locate the break in the pipes. No one knows what caused it, just one of those crazy things."

I asked if there was anything I could do.

"No. Well, yes. You could take this pitcher back to Sally Lou Parsons for me. She sent down some lemonade. Wasn't that thoughtful? Do you mind going up the hill?"

"Not a bit." Having to walk up the hill in the heat was exactly the sort of thing I wanted. Besides, it would give me a chance to see how Mrs. Parsons felt.

Mrs. Parsons opened the door herself. "Come in out of that sun, girl. It's hot."

She took the pitcher, and I followed her to the kitchen, which was all yellow and white check and looked as sunny as she did in her yellow housecoat.

"I guess you're all okay now?"

She laughed. "Me? Sure. Can't any little ole bead necklace get me down. Have some iced tea?" She poured two glasses. "We used to wear those when I was little. They're nice for summer because they're light. Don't go," she said as the telephone rang. "That's probably Mary Knapp. She calls up every blessed day to give me the dirt. I'll get rid of her."

It was flattering to think that Mrs. Parsons would rather visit with me than hear the latest gossip. I certainly wouldn't want anything to happen to her even if I didn't agree with all her ideas.

I was sipping my iced tea when I heard Mrs. Parsons exclaim, "No! No fooling! When?" I put my glass down.

"But I just saw Sylvia and Lester in a restaurant last week, and they looked perfectly happy together. What happened? You mean he just said he was leaving her for no reason?"

I felt in the way. I started toward the door.

"Wait," Mrs. Parsons called, and said into the telephone, "I've got somebody here. I'll call you back."

She hung up and told me the Ortons were getting a divorce. "It was *his* idea. Mary Knapp says *she's* just heart-broken. And I feel so sorry for those kids! Both away at camp and how are they gonna feel when they come home! Sit down and finish your tea."

I said it was delicious, but I felt like going for a swim. Mrs. Parsons went with me to the door. "Thanks for bringing my pitcher. One of these days you and I are going to the village and have us an ice-cream soda."

The nicer she was, the worse I felt. And the news about the Ortons was depressing. It was worse than what had happened to Mrs. Parsons and Mr. Hillyer. You couldn't get over a divorce in just a few days. Was this more of Meeghan's mischief?

And what about the Orton kids? Would they have to leave the lake? Would they have to choose between their father and mother? Or would some judge choose for them?

I walked home slowly, ambled down to the water's edge and stood there, picking up small stones and bits of crumbled cement and throwing them in to hear them plunk. What if *I* had to decide? I liked both my parents. There were girls at school who said they hated their father or mother, sometimes both. Usually because a parent was unfair or too strict.

"My older sister got pregnant in high school," one girl said, "and now my father watches me like a hawk and makes me get home by eleven. He doesn't trust me. I hate him." Another girl said, "They let my brother drive the car and stay out late, but not me. It isn't fair. I hate them both."

That kind of talk surprises me. My parents aren't perfect, but I still love them. I can't imagine what I'd do if they separated. I admire Daddy a little more, maybe, but Mother's fun. I simply couldn't choose between them.

I made myself a sandwich and then looked around, wondering if there were anything I could do for anyone, as if a good deed could wipe out the harm I had done.

From the kitchen window I could see Mr. Hillyer resting on their front porch with a pillow at his back. He was in a bathrobe and looked pale. I walked over.

"How are you feeling, Mr. Hillyer?"

He smiled. "Jenny, I feel as if I were getting over the worst hangover I ever had. But I'll live. How are things with you? I saw you at the game, cheering for Shawn Denihee, you traitor. We men will have to get our own cheerleader."

"I was not! I wasn't cheering for Shawn. I was cheering for all the boys."

Mr. Hillyer raised one eyebrow, brought the other down. "What's wrong with Shawn? I had him in algebra last year, and I thought he was a pretty good kid."

"He may have been okay then, but . . ."

"I hope he can come back. They need him on the basketball team. Shawn's marks were down, you know, and his parents felt he might do better in a small school where he could get more individual attention. Our classes are too big, it's true."

It had never occurred to me that Shawn had been sent to private school because of his grades. "And *is* he doing better?"

"So his mother says. Of course, there are no *distractions* at Talcott. It's a boys' school." Mr. Hillyer gave me a wink and then put his head back as if he were tired.

"Well, I hope you feel better."

I walked on with no special destination in mind. A new notice had been tacked to the bulletin board.

> *Due to petty vandalism, children are not allowed in the upstairs rooms of the clubhouse. Boys and girls are limited to the locker rooms until further notice.*

Fine thing, I thought. Something happens, they always blame the kids. Petty vandalism! Who'd want a dopey old picture of the club officers! Mr. Walsh, Mr. Pettit, and all.

As I stood glaring at the notice, Mrs. Hillyer drove up in her car. "Want a lift up the hill, Jenny?"

"No, thanks. I just came from there. I was talking to Mr. Hillyer. He seems fine."

She nodded and pointed to a bag of groceries beside her. "He's going to hate me when he sees what I've bought for him—baby food. But the doctor wants him on a very bland diet for a few days. And it's his own fault."

I was interested. "How do you mean?"

"He was behind Russell Pettit in the line at the cook-out, and when Russell stopped to joke with someone, Bill just reached around and grabbed Russell's serving." She sighed. "It was rough there, for a while, but in a way I guess it was lucky. Bill's so much younger. Mr. Pettit might not have been able to throw it off so easily at his age."

The poisoned shish-kebab had been meant for Mr. Pettit. Mr. Hillyer had got it instead.

When Mrs. Hillyer had gone, I looked again at the notice on the bulletin board. Everything was suddenly clear. It was Meeghan who had taken the picture from the clubhouse. I had seen Pookie playing with a frame. Mr. Pettit was a club officer. Meeghan had wanted his photograph so she could perform certain rites over it.

But Meeghan had made a mistake. Was she just careless? Or was she a beginner, still learning the craft?

My breath came hard. If Meeghan was a novice, then she could still choose. What was it I had read in that book on black magic? "The turning point in a witch's career comes early. While still a novice, she must choose for good or evil." Meeghan was pretty young. She could easily be just a beginner.

I marched to the Matthews' house and banged the knocker.

"Come in, Jenny," Meeghan called, as if she'd been expecting me. "Anything wrong?"

She was in the porch swing, one foot on the floor propelling her back and forth, a book in her hands. I looked her full in the face.

"Mr. Hillyer was poisoned by an oleander stick. It got into the meat of his shish-kebab. He wouldn't have got it, but he reached around Mr. Pettit and took it. That was a mistake, wasn't it?"

Meeghan gave me a charming smile. "Nobody's perfect."

I couldn't help smiling. "That oleander was from your garden."

"Could be. I have some. I got the bush from Mr. Walsh. He has several bushes. He was taking some out to make room for a dogwood tree."

"Oh." Could I have been mistaken?

"Everybody makes mistakes." Meeghan stuck out her stomach, and even her face looked fat, somehow. "That's why they put those little red things on the end of pencils, ha ha ha."

I burst out laughing. It was a perfect imitation of Mr. Pettit.

"Meeghan, you're *terrible*. How did you do it?" I'm always amazed when some actor on TV can sound exactly like someone else.

"Just concentrate on the person. Let the sight and sound of him fill your whole mind," Meeghan said. "The rest is easy."

Afterwards, I wondered if Meeghan might have been talking about the way to put a spell or a hex on someone. At the time, I thought she was telling how to do imitations.

"Do it again."

She shook her head, put a cigarette between her lips, and went to the living room looking for matches, which she found in the little desk.

"Did I ever show you this?"

She gave me a newspaper clipping, brown with age, its corners crumbled away. It showed a clown on the seat of a circus wagon pulled by six little donkeys."

"Your grandfather? I thought he did juggling."

"In those days people with small circuses did a little bit of everything. Played in the band if they could. Rode in the parade. Grandfather had a way with horses. They'd do anything for him. Grandmother told fortunes."

Meeghan struck a match on the top of the stone table.

"That's a gravestone, isn't it?" I said. "I guess you found that over on the hill where you got the myrtle."

"Somebody's started to plough up that hill," Meeghan said. "I thought I might as well put it to use." It seemed to me a practical and sensible thing. And it certainly made a good table top.

Meeghan outlined the letters with her forefinger. "R.I.P. *Requiescat in Pace*. You know what that means, of course. Do you take Latin?"

"No, I'm taking Spanish. But I can guess. Rest in peace?"

"Right. Quite a coincidence, isn't it?"

Another one of her puzzling remarks. I let it go because I saw my father's car go by. "I'd better be getting home."

She waved to me from the door.

I was half-way home when it hit me: R.I.P. stood for Russell I. Pettit as well as Rest in Peace. What was she planning for him? And what had she done to *me?* I had gone there with the firm intention of having a showdown, confronting her with her wicked actions, and had ended up being buddies.

Perhaps she had enchanted me.

TWELVE

Good witch or bad? Or some kind of enchantress? There were times in the next few days when I longed for someone to talk to. Someone my own age, that is.

To call Diane in Maine would cost a year's allowance, with all the explaining I'd have to do. I thought of Shawn. But when you've pointedly snubbed someone, as I had that day on the float, you can't just call up and say, "Hi."

So it was up to me alone. I'd try again before Meeghan went too far. One evening I set out for the Matthews', practicing all the way. "Meeghan," I'd say, "I know you're a witch, so tell me, as a friend, if you are practicing Black Magic or the 'old religion.' Otherwise . . ."

Otherwise, what? "Otherwise, I'll have to expose you."

Nearing the house, I almost lost my courage. No matter what Meeghan had done, I couldn't help liking her. The very sight of her crooked smile, the sound of her husky voice, her amber-flecked green eyes brimming with mischief made me want to laugh. I amended my threat. "Of course, if you promise not to do anything really bad, I'll keep quiet."

At the door I took a deep breath and knocked, too busy rehearsing my speech to notice that the car was gone.

Niobe opened the door. Her mother and father would be right back. They'd just gone to meet the train. "Dolores is coming. She's going to stay all week. Maybe two. She's on vacation."

Dolores, I discovered the next day, was Mr. Matthews' mother—a small, neat person with a pixie hair cut, strangely youthful for a grandmother. Every day that week she and Meeghan could be seen flying by in the Matthews' old yellow convertible.

"Going to an auction," Meeghan would call out, passing me in the car. "Taking Dolores to the Art Gallery," or, ". . . to the Farmer's Market."

There was no chance to talk to Meeghan, which was really a relief. I wasn't looking forward to a show-down with her. And Meeghan was not likely to do anything really wicked while her mother-in-law was visiting. Mr. Matthews was on vacation, too. I would see them all sitting around an umbrella table they had set up near the garden—talking and laughing and having great fun. For me, it was a kind of reprieve.

I swam, dove, baby-sat, read books, went shopping with Mother, bought a new bathing suit. The books on witchcraft were hidden away in my bureau, forgotten. I told myself everything was all right. Mr. Hillyer was up and walking around now. Mrs. Parsons was fine and back at the beach. The caterpillars were gone. (Daddy said they'd gone into a chrysalis stage, but at least they were out of sight.) The leaves were coming back on the trees. Things were back to normal—except for the Ortons' divorce, which was definite. Mother said she was glad to see I'd stopped frowning.

At night, however, I dreamed of witches. I saw them lighting fires, waving broomsticks. One night I saw six of them standing in a circle, their long robes held out in their joined hands like a curtain. I didn't want to see what was behind that curtain; it would be something dreadful, I knew. But something made me look. Two figures were dancing and shrieking with silent laughter—one had long blond hair, the other was only half-human, with cloven hoofs and a bearded, horned face.

I awoke shivering and from then on could not keep this vision out of my head. I took a swim before breakfast and lay down in the sun, trying to remember things Diane and I had done when we were little.

Making dandelion curls was one. I picked a dandelion, split the stem with my fingernail, and sucked it

until the two halves curled down in tight curls. How had we stood the taste when we were small? It was bitter, bitter as poison. I spit it out, drank some milk, and ate a big breakfast. Afterwards, I walked to the mail boxes at the foot of the hill, telling myself there wouldn't be any mail. There never is when you make a special trip.

But there was. A letter and some bills for Daddy. Two postcards for me. One from Diane showed a picture of a lighthouse. "The water up here feels like crushed ice cubes. Help!" The other card was from Paul Green and showed the mountains of Boulder. "Scenery here terrific. I guess it will be the University of Colorado for me." So he'd be way out there. But he still had another year of high school.

It was Mother's day off. She came out of the bedroom in leotards. She once had studied ballet and still likes to do barre work sometimes.

"Any mail?"

"Two postcards for me and a letter for Daddy." It was addressed to M. Sterling Henderson. "Does Daddy have another first name?"

"That stands for Monsieur, silly," Mother said, when I showed her the envelope. "That must be from his French teacher. Leave it on the hall table where he'll see it when he comes in."

We always get something good to eat on Mother's day off—because she does enjoy doing special things. She was making *coq au vin*. It smelled so good I could hardly wait for dinner time. Mother's recipe calls for browning the chicken pieces in butter and then baking it with white wine, mushrooms, and little seedless grapes. We were in the kitchen when we heard the front door close.

"Hi, Sterling. Hot in town?" Mother called.

"What?" Daddy was in the hall looking through the mail.

"I just said, was it hot in town?"

"Not too bad."

"Is that from Madame Vartan?"

"What?" He was busy with his letter now.

"Is your letter from your French teacher?"

He stuffed it into his pocket. "No, it's from Lisa Hillyer. We're writing to each other in French, for practice. What are you making? Smells good."

A few days later Meeghan telephoned. Dolores had left. Did I remember I had promised to baby-sit for them?

"I'll be there." The date brought me down to earth. It was the date they had circled on their calendar, the most important date in the witch's year. It was the chance I'd been looking for.

I sat on the porch, waiting for it to be time to go, planning my attack. "Hi, Jenny," Meeghan would say. I'd look her right in the eyes. "*Happy Lammas!*"

Meeghan would look surprised. Then she'd smile. "So you know about Lammas, do you?" Yes, and that's not all I know. I know you're a witch, and the rest of the family are witches, too. Or else they're bewitched. I know you caused all the trouble here. Oh, I admit I enjoyed it—at first. But you've gone too far. I never wanted people poisoned and divorced.

"No. You just wanted them eaten by tiny red ants," she might say.

"I was just angry. I didn't mean it."

Oh, yes you did. It was the voice of my conscience speaking. The night of the annual meeting, if you'd been able to point a finger at everyone on the Committee and say *Die*, you would have.

To get rid of the voice, I opened a book. But it was too dark to read. White moths fluttered everywhere, their delicate wings twinkling against the dark tree trunks. Mother said they were gypsy moths. They had come from the cocoons that clung to the sides of our house and the bark of the trees. They would lay their eggs in the bark, and a whole new crop of caterpillars would infest our trees and bushes next summer. Unless something were done.

"They look pretty, though," I said to Mother.

"They may look pretty, but they cause a lot of trouble."

It was nearly nine. I walked through the living room. My parents were in their usual places on the love seat. Daddy with a book in his hands and his thick French dictionary in his lap, Mother with her feet on the coffee table, reading and knitting at the same time. They stay home a lot, doing just that, and don't seem to mind. In fact, I've heard mother say often, after some party or other affair, that her favorite times are when they just sit reading that way.

"Tell Mrs. Matthews I said hello," Mother said as I left. But I was going to say *Happy Lammas*.

Clouds of moths drifted before me, like pale flowers freed from their stems, as I walked down the road. It was hard to remember that pretty things could do harm.

Happy Lammas, I practiced.

The Matthews' house was dark, but the tiny fires of lighted cigarette ends showed that they were on the screened porch. A murmur of voices told me they had guests. I was disappointed. I couldn't say anything in front of company.

The guests proved to be the Wilsons. They were just taking a walk around the lake and had stopped by for a minute. They were all talking about the Brooks, the people who had created a stir by turning the club down.

"I understand Mrs. Brook objected to our policy of 'screening' people," Mr. Wilson said. "That kind of thing gives the lake a bad reputation. A lot of people here are quite liberal. That's what Pettit doesn't realize. His ideas are out-of-date and were wrong to begin with. We ought to get him off that committee."

"I don't suppose he'd resign," Meeghan said.

Ordinarily this kind of conversation would bore me. But not tonight.

"Not a chance," Mr. Wilson said. "He's been chairman of that committee since Lincoln was a little boy."

"You might try what they do in business—kick him upstairs," Mr. Matthews suggested. "You know: give him a fancy title, and put him where he can't do any harm."

"The only place that man can't do any harm," Mrs. Wilson said, "is in the grave. And I'm not even sure about that!"

Everyone laughed. I laughed, too. Then I remembered how Meeghan had traced his initials on the stone table top and gave a little shudder.

A moment later the Wilsons left, and I saw that Meeghan and Mr. Matthews were going to leave themselves. Meeghan was wearing a kind of tunic, I noticed, as they went through the lighted living room.

"It's for dancing," she said, at the door.

"Yes," I said. "It is Lammas, isn't it?"

"What? Oh, yes. Lammas. And the Age of Aquarius." And they were gone, leaving me with another riddle. Her attitude told me nothing. It had been gay.

For once, the children were in bed. I turned on the television set and snapped it off again, feeling unsettled. My thoughts were whirling around like artificial snow in a paperweight. Were they celebrating Lammas, going to a witch's esbat? Or just to a dance?

For the millionth time the arguments started in my head. Wasn't there a natural explanation for everything that had happened? Other places had caterpillar plagues. Other people ate things and got sick, had water pipes break, got divorced. *They* didn't blame witchcraft. Meeghan might just be a far-out character having fun.

Of course, she was different. That was what I liked about her. I even liked the house—in a way—better than I had before. Anybody could go to a store and buy furniture. Meeghan had assembled hers from junk shops or auctions or something. I liked Mr. Matthews and Pookie. And I liked Niobe, though she was independent as a cat. She was popular enough now. Little girls called for her every day. Heaven only knew what horrible and fascinating games she was teaching them!

I peeked into the kitchen. Nicky was in his cage and quiet, like the children. There was a book on the kitchen table, slender as a books of poems. *Tripping with Mushrooms*. It was illustrated with pen drawing of various types of fungi. The text described mushrooms that caused "trips"—dreams in wild colors and hallucinations. The last few pages dealt with *Amanita verna* mushrooms, which "cause the liver to deteriorate rapidly, violent pain, and in most cases death."

I snapped the book shut. Meeghan was a "black" witch. She had chosen the side of evil. How had I ever doubted it? Mushrooms. Hadn't she done enough harm? Two people had been poisoned already. She was going to try again. Poor Mr. Pettit. It was awful, awful!

And then a still more horrible thought struck me. What if she meant them for the whole committee? Meeghan had gone from silly pranks and minor discomforts, like poison ivy, to deeds that were more and more serious. What if she planned now to afflict the whole committee at once? For some of them it could prove fatal.

There were five on the committee. Mr. Pettit, Mrs. Parsons, Mrs. Orton, Mr. Hillyer, and . . .

My father.

THIRTEEN

MY FATHER WAS THE FIFTH MEMBER of the committee. Did Meeghan know he wasn't like the rest of them? Anyway, she made mistakes.

Now I really had to take action. I had to warn him and everyone else. But who would believe me? Not Daddy. He loved facts; to him, anything based on conjecture was pure nonsense. Mother at least knew there were people who *claimed* to be witches. Maybe I could tell her. I dialed our number.

"Mother?"

"Yes, Jenny."

"Hi." Now that I had her I didn't know how to begin.

"What is it, Jen? Is anything wrong?"

"No. Not really."

It was comforting to hear her voice. Even the slight note of impatience, as if she had had to stop knitting in the middle of a row, made me feel at home. Daddy never liked answering the phone either. It meant putting down that twelve-pound French dictionary or the equally heavy volume SARS to SORC of the encyclopedia.

"Everything's O.K.," I said, feeling momentarily safe. I could close my eyes and be home, sprawled by the doors leading to the upper porch while my parents sat reading in their usual places.

"Are you sure? Your voice sounds funny."

"It's just this program I was watching," I invented. "It's about this witch who looks like a plain person, so nobody will believe that she . . ."

"I don't think you should watch things like that. You're too impressionable. Aren't there some nice books you can read?"

"Listen, Mother: remember that witch in *Life* magazine? Well, what if there was a witch here, like that, causing all kinds of trouble? You've got to admit that bad things have happened lately, and all to members of the Membership Committee. People getting poisoned, and Mr. Orton wanting a divorce . . ."

"Jenny, being on a membership committee is not grounds for divorce in any state, as yet. Why don't you see if you can find something funny to read? Or look at a magazine?" Mother was about to hang up.

"Put Daddy on."

"He's not here."

"Not *there?*" It was like saying the roof wasn't there. "Where is he?"

"At the movies."

"At the *movies!* Daddy's gone to the movies *alone?*"

"No, with Mrs. Hillyer. She's in his French class, you know. It's a French film without English subtitles. I knew I wouldn't get anything out of it."

I felt too disturbed to go on talking. I hung up and stood scowling in the hall. Daddy had been so absorbed in that letter from Mrs. Hillyer he hadn't even heard when Mother spoke to him. Daddy had said Mrs. Hillyer ought to be on the Membership Committee. He loaned her books and drove her to French class. But there was something else.

Something Daddy had said earlier in the summer had struck me as false and stuck in my mind. It was after that first meeting. Mother had said something about Lisa being cute or smart. And Daddy had said, "She isn't really pretty." It had sounded unnatural and uncalled for (who had said she *was?*), even at the time. For once Daddy hadn't sounded sincere.

I sat down on the sofa. My heart was pounding. I could hear it in my ears—beat, beat, beat.

Mrs. Hillyer was interested in the same subjects Daddy was. They were serious-minded, both of them. Mother wasn't like that. She would study Spanish—but only if she were going to Spain. Daddy would study Spanish or Swahili—just to add to his knowledge. Mother picked up papers for the sake of her figure;

Daddy, as a public service. Mother liked swimming and dancing. Daddy liked tennis and skating. Mother liked music; Daddy was tone deaf.

Mother loved the ballet. Daddy refused to go watch a bunch of men flit around in ruffles and tights. I remembered them quarreling about it. They probably quarreled often, out of my hearing. It was amazing their marriage had lasted this long. They were probably only staying together for my sake.

The Hillyers didn't agree, either. Lisa had said so at the anual meeting: "Bill and I don't agree on this." Like Daddy, she was against prejudice.

I sat back and stared unseeing at the high, peaked ceiling. Probably everybody knew about it but me. What about Mother? How innocent she had sounded on the phone! But now things were coming to a head. *Something* had happened to make Daddy and Lisa start to correspond, to decide to go out together . . .

Daddy wasn't like Mr. Orton. He would never (normally) do anything to hurt Mother or me. What (or who) had changed him? Was it all part of a plan: poison for two, divorce for two, and for Mr. Pettit . . . heaven knew what?

I had a headache from thinking about it and went looking for aspirin. On the back rim of the basin in the bathroom, there was a bottle of red capsules. On the back of the toilet, a dish of chocolates! In the medicine cabinet, a bottle labeled aspirin. But I thought I'd better not chance taking *anything* in that house. I drank a

glass of water and went back to the living room. Was there anything funny to read? Mother had suggested a magazine. I spotted one in an old coal scuttle by the fire-place. A *New Yorker* several years old. I took it to the sofa.

Toward the back of the magazine, a match had been inserted. The magazine fell open to that place—an article on spiders. I wasn't going to read it; I was going to look at the cartoons, but certain words flew out at me: "severe abdominal pain . . . nausea . . ."

It wasn't fiction, but a factual account of the experience of a man who had almost died from the bite of a black widow spider. He had been hospitalized for months and not expected to live. The bite had produced nausea, vomiting, high fevers, delirium, and excruciating pain. I closed my eyes tight.

My hands were shaking. My breath came hard. It was horrible to think of anyone suffering that way. After a moment I gave a cautious glance at the magazine, as if I expected a spider to crawl from the pages. Why had this particular issue, years old, been kept? Why was the place marked with a match? I threw it from me.

The door opened, and Mr. Matthews came in.

"Meeghan will be here in a . . ."

I didn't wait to be paid but pushed past him and ran home. It was later than I had realized. My parents were in their room with the door closed. I was about to rush in, to throw myself into Mother's arms, when I heard Daddy's voice.

"Don't be ridiculous, Amy!"

"I'm not!" Mother's voice was muffled, as if her face were in the pillow. "I'm not. You said you'd be back at . . . muffle, muffle . . . sitting here alone . . .

muffle, muffle, . . . never see you again!"

"You're being childish."

I didn't want to hear any more. I ran to my own room and held a pillow over my ears. I didn't want them to separate! I didn't want to have to choose! I didn't want to leave the lake.

Even after I fell asleep, I could feel my head throbbing, threatening to wake me from the dreams to which I had escaped and send me back to reality.

FOURTEEN

MOTHER LOOKED TIRED in the morning. I must have looked awful myself, for she said she didn't want me to baby-sit for the Matthews any more—they kept me too late.

It was Saturday. Daddy was mowing the lawn. Mother was getting ready to go to the shop. She had to work half a day, but she didn't seem to mind. She would probably be glad to get away. I let my cereal grow soggy. My parents' quarrel had been a shock. But I couldn't worry about that now. There was the threat of the Amanita mushroom to think about and that of the Black Widow spider.

The club supper was only two weeks off. Some of the women would make casseroles, some desserts, others salads. Meeghan would send something made with mushrooms. Someone would get violently ill. And finally, Russell Pettit (or someone else, if Meeghan made a mistake) would be bitten by a spider and suffer unbearable pain. And perhaps die.

I would see to it that my parents didn't attend that supper. I'd pretend to be ill myself, have hysterics, something. But that wasn't enough. I really had to see that Meeghan's whole plan failed. And I had no idea how to do it.

I was willing to expose Meeghan now, but I was convinced that no one would believe me. Not even Mother. She might concede that there were "so-called" witches in Los Angeles. But such things didn't happen *here*.

Could I talk to Meeghan herself? Plead with her? "Look, Meeghan, I know I once talked about torture and slow death, but that was crazy. These people aren't bad. They just have mistaken ideas. And we can't change their ideas by hurting them. So would you please call the whole thing off?"

Oh, sure. "Call what off?" she might ask. She had never admitted being a witch. She would probably just give an amused smile and make some puzzling remark.

"Don't sit there dreaming, Jenny," Mother's voice broke into my thoughts. "I want you to eat something nourishing. Have an egg." She was ready to leave.

"I will. In a minute." I followed her outside. "Mother, who's in charge of the covered-dish supper?"

"Mrs. Orton. Why?"

"Mrs. Orton! I thought she was getting a divorce."

"Yes. And Mr. Orton has left. But she has to stay here until she can sell the house. Mrs. Walsh wanted to relieve her of the job of running the supper, but the others felt it would be good for her. Keep her mind busy, you know."

Yes, I do know, I thought, my throat growing hard. Like you, not minding going to work today.

"Why did you want to know about the supper?" Mother asked.

"I thought I might help." I said.

Mother turned around to stare at me. She couldn't have been more surprised if I had offered to straighten my closet.

"Help serve. I thought it might be fun. It would be experience in case I wanted to work in a restaurant," I improvised. "They say you get big tips."

"Well, you can ask." Mother slammed the car door. "See you later. I'll be home early."

Mrs. Orton wasn't as surprised as Mother had been. "Well, aren't you nice!" She was painting shutters, a cap pulled over her gray-blond hair to keep the paint out.

But the covered-dish suppers were always served buffet-style. The food was set out on a long table and people helped themselves.

"Maybe I could help out in the kitchen. Don't you need somebody to carry the stuff upstairs?"

It had come to me that I could inspect each casserole and, when I found one made with mushrooms, manage to drop it. But everything was arranged, she told me. People brought casseroles from home. They were kept hot in the clubhouse oven, and the caretaker brought everything up on big trays. Mrs. Orton was afraid I would just be in his way.

"But it's certainly sweet of you to offer." Mrs. Orton fanned herself with her cap and sat down on the porch steps, looking carefully behind her. "I never sit down now without looking," she grinned. "I don't know if you heard what happened when I painted my bathroom . . ."

"Yes, I did. You're going to move away?"

"Yes. And I'm lucky. I've just found a little apartment in Deerwood. Small, but convenient. I'm going to work full-time now in an insurance office there. I can still show houses weekends and continue my real estate business." She put on her cap and went back to painting.

"What about Lynn and Steven?"

"Lynn will be back in college. Stevie will have to go to private school. I'll see them during vacations. But the main thing is getting this house ready and on the market. It's awful to have to think about money all the time, isn't it?"

She was certainly being a good sport, with her whole life changing. "But if you don't live here, you and Lynn and Steven won't be able to come swimming. Except once in a while as guests. We've got all those dopey signs saying *Private. Keep Out.*"

Mrs. Orton took off a painting glove to tuck a strand of hair under her cap. "They're not 'dopey,' Jenny. The people who spent their money to buy property here at Clover Lake did so because they wanted to get away from the crowds in the city. If we didn't have those signs, there'd be no room on the beach for the people who pay for it."

I'd never thought of that. But I didn't have time to stand and talk. I said good-by to Mrs. Orton and went on. The trees were still. There was no breeze. It was hot.

The Pettit's house is a Cape Cod type, its shingles stained gray. It's set against the woods with a lawn in front and a garden on one side. Mrs. Pettit, in a wide straw hat, was tying tall plants to stakes with raffia.

"Hello, Jenny. What can I do for you?" Without waiting for an answer, she went on to say they were going away for a few days and wanted to leave everything in order. "Some friends in Florida have been begging us to come down, so we thought we'd run down for a week or so while the rates are low."

They certainly had a beautiful garden. The flowers ranged from tall delphinium against the house down to low petunias, pink and white and rose.

"Were you looking for my hubby?"

"Not exactly." I hadn't planned what to say.

"I thought maybe you had a message from your father."

"Oh, yes. I do. He asked me to tell people living up here near the woods to be careful and watch out for Black Widow spiders. He heard there were a lot of them around. You know what they look like? They have a mark the shape of an hour-glass on the underside."

"Thank you, dear. I'll be careful."

"Well, you'd better warn Mr. Pettit. The bite can be fatal. He does a lot of work around, doesn't he? He'd better not reach under logs or rocks or woodpiles or anything. In fact, he ought to stay out of the woods."

She smiled. "That's what I keep telling him. He does too much, at his age. Especially in winter. But there aren't any boys big enough to shovel snow any more. They're all off at college, or else they're too small."

"Don't I know!"

"Sophie! Sophie!" Mr. Pettit came from behind the house. One hand was bright red. My heart turned over. I was too late.

He held the hand up. "Hello, there, Jenny. Isn't this a sight? It's that damned poison ivy—excuse my French. I can't stop scratching, so Sophie put mercurochrome on to keep it from getting infected."

It had been a shock. I sank down on the porch step. Mrs. Pettit brought me a glass of water. When I'd finished it, I held the cold glass against my right temple and then my left.

"Feeling better?" she asked. "I'll bet you ran up the hill. Shouldn't do that in this heat."

Mr. Pettit cut some flowers—blue delphinium, crimson phlox, pink and white larkspur. They looked pretty together. "Take these home to your mother."

I thanked them and left. I really felt like a crumb.

I walked home. Well, I thought, so much for prevention. Now what?

My mind was swinging like a pendulum. I had to tell; I couldn't tell. Meeghan was wicked; I liked her. If you befriend the wicked, does that make you wicked, too? If you can prevent a crime and don't, does that make you a criminal?

"An impossible situation," I kept saying. "Impossible."

I took a swim to cool off, but the water was tepid. Clover Lake isn't very deep, and during a hot spell the water feels almost warm. I made some egg salad sandwiches from eggs Mother had cooked before leaving for work and sat in the shade trying to keep cool. Daddy was clipping the bushes.

After a while I heard the car. Mother was home. She might believe me if I hit just the right note. She had believed that story her housemother had told her at boarding school about the woman with second sight being able to foretell the future.

Yes, Mother might believe me. But if she did, and she convinced Mrs. Walsh and the others that Meeghan was practicing witchcraft, what would they do? In the old days witches were burned at the stake, drowned by dunking, and stoned. Nowadays they might have her arrested. At the very least, they would get signatures on a petition asking her to leave.

Mother came out of the house with the flowers and a bowl of fruit. "Had your lunch? Who sent the flowers?"

"Mr. Pettit." I sat at the table and took a little bunch of grapes from the fruit bowl. If the grapes came out even, I thought, eating a couple, I would tell. There were ten. I took a deep breath.

"Mother, so many bad things have happened lately. Doesn't it almost seem as if this place were bewitched? I mean, first the caterpillar plague, then . . ."

"It certainly does. You'd think we were under some evil spell."

"Oh, come on, now!" Daddy walked over. I guess he had been listening. "What nonsense! That's like these people who blame the space program if we have a lot of rain. We had rainy summers when I was a boy, long before the first space capsule was thought of."

"She didn't mean it that way." Mother defended me. "But you must admit that when all sorts of troubles hit at once . . ."

"That's women for you!" Daddy said. "There's a perfectly natural explanation for everything that happens, but will they believe it? No. They'd *rather* believe in the supernatural."

"We do have more imagination." Mother was keeping cool, but her cheeks were red. "We have open minds. We're willing to concede that there may be something beyond what can be proved with figures and statistics."

Daddy made a sound of disgust and pulled out a

chair. I was on Mother's side, yet in a way I hoped Daddy was right. But my greatest concern was that I had got them quarreling again.

"Look here, Sterling. You're always pointing out that drawing, the making of pictures, is a basic, natural instinct because primitive man drew on caves and all small children have the urge to draw. Well, people everywhere have always believed in the supernatural. And they still do today. Doesn't that . . ."

The argument was cut off by the ringing of the telephone. I dashed inside, though I didn't expect it to be for me. It was Mrs. Dickson, the librarian.

"Jenny, a couple of books have been turned in that I thought might interest you. One is a very nice novel called *The White Witch*. The other is a play called *Bell, Book and Candle*."

A funny title. "Is *that* about witches?"

"It's about a beautiful witch who falls in love. The title refers to a method of exorcising witches."

"A method of *what?*"

"Exorcism. Driving out evil spirits. It was done at first by the Apostles, but later it was done by ordinary laymen to rid witches of their power."

"Exorcism. Thanks, Mrs. Dickson. Thanks a lot."

I suddenly remembered having read something of the kind in *Black Magic and White*. I dashed upstairs, looked in the index, and found, "Exorcism. Method of, p. 271." On page 271, I read: "Of the various methods of exorcism (the driving out of evil spirits), the one most favored for ridding a witch of her powers entails a reading from the Bible by candlelight, followed by the ringing of bells. The Book is closed, and the candle quenched. It is believed that the holy words of the Bible bring forth the wicked powers (or evil spirits), which merge with the candle smoke and evaporate. Bells, or a single bell, are then rung in celebration of the cleansing. This ritual is usually performed by a priest, but, in the absence of a member of the clergy, may be done by a layman."

It could be done by an ordinary laymen. Someone outside the clergy. A plain person. Like me.

FIFTEEN

EXORCISM. It was the only solution. I didn't feel worthy of the job—I hadn't been to Sunday School all summer. But there was no one else to do it.

Book, bell, and candle. The book was easy—I had my own Bible. And Mother had a little tea bell that had come from a monastery in California. It was engraved with a lion, a lamb, a cross, and a serpent. It would do nicely. My problem was the candle. I couldn't use any ordinary one. And they didn't burn candles in our church.

Votive candles, I knew, could be bought in the five-and-ten. But I wanted one that had been burned in a church. Several families at Clover Lake went to the Catholic church, but I didn't know any of them well enough to make such a strange request.

There was Shawn, of course. My cheeks burned at the thought of asking him a favor. One of the hardest things in the world is asking a favor of someone you haven't been nice to. But in a way, the difficulty seemed right. The task *should* be hard.

The heat grew more intense. The sky darkened. Thunder rolled, and the rain came down. Good. You can't caddy in the rain. Shawn would be coming back from the golf course. The rain stopped as suddenly as it had started, but Daddy said it would probably rain again. There was a strange, intense light on everything. I ran down to the clubhouse between showers to wait.

At last, Shawn came loping along. I waved, and he came over to stand by the porch railing. He didn't look like a prep school student today. His clothes were wrinkled and dusty. I guess he had got a lift only part way. He looked, in fact, like a farmer. His red hair was dark with sweat, but his eyes were as blue as the lake behind him.

"How do you like Talcott?" I asked, stalling, for I didn't know how to begin.

He shrugged. "It's O.K. But it's old, you know. The buildings are kind of run-down, not new like the school here. The kids are O.K., too, only most of them are there because they have lousy marks like mine." Shawn laughed. "Or because they've been kicked out of other schools, or because their parents can't stand them or are getting divorced."

I caught my breath. Maybe *I'd* have to go away to school, like Steve Orton. "Shawn," I said quickly, "can you get me a candle from your church? One that's been lighted?"

"Sure." He didn't even ask why I wanted it.

"Will it be all right? I mean, you won't get in trouble?"

"Nah. I'll just put a new one in its place. We'll be going to nine o'clock mass. Want me to bring it around afterwards?"

"No. I'll meet you here."

He nodded as if he understood that if I wanted a burned candle for some crazy reason, I wouldn't want my parents asking questions.

"O.K. See you around ten-twenty."

"Fine." Should I have explained? Or apologized? It didn't seem necessary.

If it hadn't been for the old yew, gnarled and bent and gray, I wouldn't have found the place. The devil's beard weed was almost hidden now by barberry, bittersweet, and sassafras. The knoll was grown up with purple thistle, grapevines, and wild azalea. The grass in the circle had a flattened look. Did Meeghan and her coven meet here? Or was it only Niobe and her friends, trampling it down, playing witches?

I felt silly coming here to perform this ceremony. I had never believed in the devil or in evil powers or witches. But here I was with my Bible, the bell, and the short candle Shawn had brought me that morning. I had waited till evening to come to the knoll. I couldn't imagine performing exorcism in broad daylight.

I knelt down and lit the candle. Night was closing in. Insects hummed in the grass. Locusts gave their monotonous threep. Katydids called and answered. Slender black clouds hid the moon.

I opened the Bible. My eye fell on Matthew 5:43. *Ye have heard that it hath been said Thou shalt love thy neighbor and hate thine enemy. But I say unto you, Love your enemies . . .*

My heart beat fast. The words were like a voice in my ear. Love your enemies. I had done just the opposite. I had hated my enemies and wished them harm. I looked back at that angry girl and wondered at her—she seemed so childish. I didn't hate any of those people, not even Mr. Pettit.

I closed the book, blew out the candle, rang the bell, a wordless petition in my heart. For a moment everything was still. Then the katydids began to argue: *Yes, she is; no, she isn't. Yes, she is; no, she isn't.* Up on the hill a dog barked, and another answered in the distance. At my elbow a tree toad went ter-whee! I turned my flashlight on him and saw his throat like a giant bubble.

Was it all nonsense? Would it do any good? Had I done the right thing? Or something foolish? It started to rain again. I ran home.

Mother was on the love seat, reading, knitting, and listening to music on a Spanish radio station. The place

beside her was empty. My heart sank. A moment later I saw Daddy working at the desk.

"Glad you got back. It's going to rain hard."

I was too tired to answer. I went upstairs feeling depressed. Wasn't I presumptuous, thinking I could drive out an evil spirit? It probably had to be done in church, even if a layman did it. And why had I chosen the knoll

of all places? The very spot where the devil's beard grew. It was probably the very last place for successful exorcism. The questions of these last few days had worn me out. I fell into bed, and the steady drumming of the rain put me to sleep at once.

Some time later I opened my eyes to a frightening silence. The rain had stopped. The house was held in a hush—the moment of stillness in which a bird stands mesmerized before a snake strikes and quenches its life. There were two rapid flashes of light, a distant, ominous rumble, and then—*crack!* the air was split with a tearing sound, followed by a deafening crash. The house shook.

I jumped up, holding my ears. In another moment the rain was pounding down again, harder than ever, overflowing the gutters, gurgling loudly down the drains. I heard my parents running around closing windows.

"What's happened?"

They didn't know. Our electricity had gone off. Inside and out, everything was black. Daddy thought the upstairs porch had collapsed or that a tree had crashed onto the roof. We peered through the windows, seeing nothing. We lit candles, mopped the wet floors, put newspaper down on the linoleum. Then we all put on robes and sat around, too wide awake to go back to bed.

The rain seethed on the bushes, splattered against the black windowpanes, clattered on the flagstones. A flash of lightning illuminated the darkness, and Daddy said, "I see what it is—our big willow is down."

"No!" Mother cried. Our house is framed by two willows. It would look all wrong with just one. In the next lightning flash I saw it, the trunk stretching out over the water, the branches sticking up like masts of a sunken ship.

"Well," Mother said, "now that we know what it is we can go back to bed. The worst thing is not knowing."

In the morning the sky had cleared. We found that the willow had only split. Only about a third of the tree had fallen. The lawn was littered with branches, the driveway strewn with twigs, leaves, and ugly black cocoons.

"We can be thankful it didn't fall on the house," Mother said.

I carried the wet towels and rags we had used for mopping out to the clothes line sinking at every step. The lawn was sodden. We went down to the water's edge to inspect the tree. The long, gaping wound was white, the fallen limb extended fifty feet into the water. Daddy said the tree men would have to lift it with a block and tackle.

Standing there at the water's edge, I noticed something strange. More of the rocks of the old stone wall were showing than usual. After so much rain it should have been the opposite. Daddy knew at once what had happened. "The dam has broken."

We jumped in the car and drove toward the clubhouse. Long before we got there, we could hear the roar of rushing water. We had to stop near the mailboxes, for cars were parked at random everywhere. Water was flowing over the road. Dozens of people were there. Water had cut through the beach and was pounding against the foundation of the clubhouse. The ground floor was flooded.

The caretaker had opened the sluice gates when the dam broke to relieve pressure on the banks, and the water was pouring over the spillway in a torrent. Some of the men had already gone off with a pick-up truck for sand and burlap bags. Others collected logs. When the truck returned, Daddy and the other men filled the bags with sand and put them in place.

By noon the clubhouse was no longer in danger. Mother and I walked home. We went down the lawn and stared numbly at our once-beautiful view. The level of the lake had gone down rapidly. For twenty feet out from our lawn, there was black ooze and slime instead of water. Half-rotted logs were exposed along with old bottles and rusted cans. Blackened stumps stood up here and there. The willow lay over the slime.

The tree men came the next morning. They didn't raise the tree with a block and tackle but waded into the ooze with their power saws and cut the limb into movable sections.

Everything was topsy-turvy. It was hard to remember what day it was or know what to do. Mrs. Wilson relieved me of my job by taking the children to her mother's for two weeks. There was no swimming. I spent most of the day watching the tree men sawing, painting the wound, and carrying huge circles of wood to the truck.

I carried the smaller pieces. When the crew left, I went on picking up twigs and small branches. There must have been thousands of them. Mother told me not to get too tired, but I had to keep on—bending, straightening, carrying. It was my fault. I had failed. The storm was one more in the series of catastrophes that Meeghan had brought about with her magic.

At dinner I ate mechanically, my back aching. Mother looked out on the lawn, confetti-dotted with chips too small for gathering. "That tree needed pruning anyway," she said. "It was beginning to block the view of the lake."

Daddy agreed. "It would have cost about the same, and we'd never have had the courage to have that much of it removed."

They were right. The willow was simply a slender version of its former self and more closely matched the tree on the other side. So that was all right.

"And as for the dam," Daddy said, "it was cracked before, but the club didn't want to pay to have it repaired. Now we'll have to build a new one, and it will be stronger and safer."

I sat up, hardly daring to believe that good had come out of the storm, but Mother was saying it was all for the best.

". . . except for one thing. The clubhouse kitchen is flooded. The covered-dish supper will have to be postponed indefinitely."

I felt better. My back was no longer tired.

"And another thing," Mother said, "that nice garden the Matthews planted was washed away. You'd think they'd know better than to plant it on a slope."

It was gone. The witch's garden had washed away.

"By the way, Jenny. I saw your friend Meeghan. I told her I was sorry about her garden and told her about our willow. As usual, I didn't know what she was talking about. 'I guess you had a power failure too,' I said. And she said, 'Does it show?' "

Mother sighed with perplexity. "Does it show! What does *that* mean!"

I almost cheered. Meeghan had had a "power failure." The exorcism had worked. I had succeeded. Not I, of course, but the book, the candle, and the bell. And something more. Something I had felt, up there on the knoll.

SIXTEEN

THE THREAT WAS OVER. Meeghan had lost her power. I was free from worry and responsibility and guilt.

Of course, the water level of the lake was still down. There was no swimming. Fish died on the muddy banks, and flies swarmed over them. But at least there would be no further poisonings, no spider bites, no more divorces.

I didn't go near the Matthews' place, for Meeghan, unless her intuition was gone, would know I had been instrumental in what had happened. Or my guilty face would tell her. So I looked over my school clothes, did some cooking, helped Daddy with the outside work. Things seemed fine between my parents.

Two days after the storm I came downstairs and saw a suitcase in the living room. "Who's going away?"

"We all are," Mother told me. She was on vacation. Daddy was through with his tutoring class. We were going away to celebrate their coming wedding anniversary.

We left for Westhampton the next morning—a three hour drive. I loved every minute, though it's really a boring trip. I love the seashore at any time, and right now it was just what I needed, for after my first elation over the success of the exorcism, I had a feeling of letdown, emptiness.

Now, suddenly, everything was wonderful. The smell of the sea air, the very feel of it on my skin, was refreshing. The blue sky was so vast, the vistas so open and wide that my old self with its fears and worries shrank to nothing. The ocean stretched further than I could see. The waves crashed endlessly on the sand, and I was reduced to proper size. All this was here long before I was born, I thought, and would go on till the end of the world.

We swam, sunbathed, and took long walks on the beach, Mother and I stopping to pick up shells, Daddy sprinting on ahead over the wet sand at the water's edge and back again. Daddy would really like to be climbing mountains, Mother told me. Lolling on a beach is too inactive a sport for him.

"You and I are the ones who love beaches," Mother said one time, looking after Daddy as he ran far out of sight, "and where do we always go for vacations? A place like this."

I'd never realized that.

The morning of their anniversary we drove to Southampton and walked down Job's Lane looking at the shops. When we came to a bookstore, we went in. Mother and Daddy often give each other books at gift time. I wanted to buy them a present and wandered back to the record department. There I had a brainstorm and picked out an Yves Montand album. Mother would enjoy the music. Daddy would enjoy translating the French.

I paid for my purchase, pleased with my clever choice. Then Daddy opened his wallet to pay for his, and my heart felt cold. There in his wallet was a sheet of lavender-blue notepaper. Lisa Hillyer's letter. He was keeping it—the way I'd kept that valentine from Shawn.

A little snatch of blue and the perfection of our vacation was gone. I wondered if Mother knew he still had that letter. Later that day, when Daddy was lost in the book she had given him, *A Treatise on French Verbs*, I eased into the subject as Mother and I walked along the beach.

"Boys never say what they mean. They say just the opposite. I'll bet grown men do the same thing."

"Possibly," Mother murmured, absently, picking up a shell.

"I was thinking—remember what Daddy said once

about Mrs. Hillyer? He said, 'She isn't really pretty.' Said it out of a clear sky. Well, I don't think he meant that. I think he meant just the opposite, but didn't want us to think he did."

Mother looked at me in surprise. "Jenny, you're growing up."

It was about time she realized it. "I think he likes her a lot."

"Yes, he does. And Lisa admires Daddy, I'm sure."

"Don't you mind?" I asked, a little exasperated with her for being so calm. "Like their going to the movies together?"

"Not when it's just once a year. We don't get French movies up our way very often. But Lord, Jenny! What a time I had that night!" Mother stood, turning the shell in her hands, brushing away the sand.

"It was my own fault, of course," she said. "I have this ridiculous imagination. Whenever Daddy's late, I'm convinced he's been in an accident. That night I was actually in tears. I said, 'I thought I'd never see you again.' I was sure they were dead in a ditch somewhere, the three of them."

"The *three* of them!"

"Yes. Daddy and Mrs. Hillyer and Madame Vartan, the French teacher. The whole class met at the theatre and then—you know how Daddy is—he insisted on driving Madame Vartan all the way home. It sounds silly now, but I tell you it was absolute torture."

I sank down on the sand near a fort some child had

left half-finished, letting the idea sink in. I had simply miscontrued what I had heard.

"What brought all this up?" Mother asked.

"Nothing. Just seeing Mrs. Hillyer's letter in Daddy's wallet."

"Tst!" Mother made a sound of impatience. "He should have answered that long ago. I keep telling him. But he's such a perfectionist! Well, maybe now with his book on verbs . . ."

Mother and I patted the walls of the fort in place. "Lisa Hillyer is attractive and very bright, too. She and Daddy have a lot in common," Mother said. "But Daddy and I have a lot more. We have you, our home, and years of shared experience. Opposites make good marriages, you know. They enrich each other. What could I learn from a person just like myself?"

Mother stuck a broken shell on top of the fort for a flag. "The Hillyers are different types, and they have a very solid marriage, too. Besides . . ." A mischievous smile curved Mother's lips. "Have you ever taken a good look at Bill Hillyer? He's awfully good looking."

I resented the comparison. "He's not as *smart* as Daddy!"

Mother laughed. "Nobody's that smart!"

We had been away eight days. The ninth day the sky was overcast for the first time, and Daddy suggested we go home. Mother agreed. "It's been wonderful. Let's not spoil it."

We drove back to Clover Lake. It seemed as if we had been gone ages. I expected people to say, "Well, welcome back!" They didn't even realize we'd been away. I expected our mailbox to be filled with letters. There was only one—for Mother. The rest was junk mail and bills.

Mother's letter was from Mrs. Holcombe. She skimmed through it. "Oh, good! They're taking a place in Deerwood this fall, so Diane won't have to change schools. Their summer cabin is all finished, and they want us to come up for a weekend sometime soon. Now are you happy, Jenny?"

"Sure," I said. But I wasn't as happy as I should have been.

Daddy stopped at the bulletin board. A notice said that the covered-dish supper had been canceled. A printed sign advertised a Teen Canteen newly-opened in Deerwood. We drove on home. The wind was blowing from the north, and the leaves made a whispery sound. They had grown thick again, as if there had never been a plague of caterpillars.

The house felt stuffy after the seashore, but only for a moment. Daddy opened the doors to the porch and then went straight to the record player and put on the record I'd given them. Mother stopped in the middle of unpacking to listen.

"Mmm! That Yves Montand! Hasn't he got the sexiest voice! I'd love to know what he's saying."

"Why don't you come to our French class next term?" Daddy suggested.

"Maybe I will."

After dinner Mr. Walsh called to ask Daddy to be chairman of the Membership Committee. The Pettits were going to spend the winter in Florida, so Mr. Pettit had resigned. Daddy accepted, provided he could have some "forward looking" people on the committee.

"Does there have to *be* a committee?" I asked, when Daddy had hung up.

He said that since any new people coming here would be joint-owners of the roads, the lake, the clubhouse, and the water system, we had to be sure they were willing to pay their share. That was all. There would certainly be no restrictions.

It was a beautiful day. I had a deep tan. We had had a wonderful vacation. There was no reason to feel depressed. I walked down the road. The trench in front of the Morrows' house had been filled in and smoothed over. The Matthews' place looked fine. The flagstones were back in place. It looked as it had when the Holcombes were living there.

Why wasn't I happier? It was still August. Goldenrod and wild asters were growing on the side of the road, but summer wasn't over yet. At the ball field Shawn and a few younger boys were practicing drop kicks. I sat down on the stone wall to watch. Shawn ran over.

"Hey! You're back! Where did you go, anyway—China?"

I laughed. It was nice that somebody had missed me.

"Did you see the sign on the bulletin board, about the Teen Canteen?" Shawn asked.

"Yes. Is it any good?"

"I don't know. I've been wanting to go, but . . . how about Saturday night? Want to try it? I could take my guitar."

"Fine! I'd like to." I hadn't even known that he played the guitar.

The boys yelled for him. He went back to the field. "See you Saturday."

I had a date. It would be nice. I really liked Shawn. I guess I always have. Diane and Richie would be coming back in September. I'd be seeing them in school every day. Everything was fine now.

Wasn't it?

SEVENTEEN

If everything was fine, why did I feel so gloomy, as if joy and laughter were gone out of my life forever, and only calm, sober, uneventful days lay ahead?

"You're growing up," Mother had said at Westhampton. But was I? Would a mature person *mind* a future that promised to be calm and serene? Surely I didn't want those enchanted times back again when I'd been so afraid.

I wondered what Meeghan was doing, now that she had lost her powers. I hadn't inquired. I was too cowardly.

One evening, about the third day after our return from Westhampton, I decided to stop by. It was ridiculous to avoid Meeghan—as if we'd had a quarrel. I waited until I thought they'd be through dinner and walked down the road. As I approached the house a car backed out of the driveway. Their yellow convertible was covered with signs of the zodiac, peace symbols, and mottoes: "Love. Peace. Make Love Not War."

"Hi, Jenny," Mr. Matthews called. "Have a nice time?"

Meeghan was wearing a flowered linen dress, very much like one Mother had. Her hair was pinned into a smooth French twist.

"Mm! Look at that gorgeous tan!" She sounded like Mrs. Parsons, giving compliments that way.

"You look nice, too," I said lamely. She had probably been to the hairdresser's—to Mr. Joseph—like Mrs. Walsh and the others. She'd be going to bridge parties next, and meetings of the P.T.A. I felt gloomier every moment.

Niobe was seated between her parents. She looked just about like the other girls at the lake, too. Her cheeks were a healthy pink, scattered becomingly with freckles. Fine thing, I said to myself.

"We're getting a dog!" Niobe told me, bouncing happily on the seat. That figures, I thought. A dog. Just like an ordinary family.

"That's nice," I said unenthusiastically. I wondered what would happen to Meeghan's rat with a dog in the house.

"What about Nicky?"

Meeghan's face clouded. "Nicky died. It was very

strange. He was perfectly all right, and one evening—it was the night of the big storm—we came in and found him dead. He couldn't have died of fright. It happened just before the storm."

I felt my cheeks grow warm. It must have happened just after I had quenched the candle and rung the bell. I looked down so she might not read the guilt in my eyes. Although I had never liked Nicky, I couldn't help sighing.

Mr. Matthews gave me a sympathetic smile. "I can see you hated to come back. It's always hard to get adjusted after vacation."

"Yes. Well, as Daddy would say, *tant pis*—too bad. You go away, and when you come back, it's just—nothing."

"Right," Meeghan agreed. "I'm with you, Jen. We were thinking of moving back to the city. But then your father asked Matt to be on the Membership Committee, and Matt wants to do it. Besides, fall is coming." She gave me a wink. "I'd hate to miss Hallowe'en in the country."

Before I could think how she meant that, Pookie appeared out of nowhere. He had been hiding in the well behind the back seat. He popped out, a grin splitting his face in two, his sun-bleached hair falling over his ears. I felt a little cheered at the sight of him. He looked as pixie-like as ever.

"We're going to have our own house to sleep in, Prince and me!" he announced. "A green one!"

Prince! Were they going to call the dog Prince? That would be just too much.

"This is Prince," Pookie said, holding up a frog.

"I said *Prince* could sleep in the greenhouse," Meeghan corrected. "*You'll* sleep in your own room. Pook thinks his frog may be a prince under a spell," she explained, "and wants to treat him with respect."

"You're getting a greenhouse?" I asked. That was something nobody had at the lake.

"Just a small one. The kind you put together yourself," Mr. Matthews told me. "Plexiglass and a metal frame. Meeghan didn't feel she could wait till spring to start another garden."

Meeghan nodded. "I want to try growing some herbs. Angelica and sage and rue . . ."

I caught my breath. Angelica and sage and rue were beneficial herbs, the kind used by good witches for ointments and healing. Was it possible, after all, that Meeghan had been at the beginning of her career when we met? A novice, able to choose for good or evil? The words of the book on black magic and white were as clear as if printed on the air before my eyes. ". . . at this moment her choice may be influenced by . . . the phases of the moon, the position of the stars . . . or by an outsider."

Mr. Matthews put the car in gear. Pookie, standing on the back seat, leaning forward, began pulling hairpins from his mother's hair and throwing them away. Instead of scolding him, Meeghan smiled, and I noticed

for the first time that one of her front teeth was crooked. It only made her smile more bewitching.

"Stop in later," she said. "We'll mix up a love potion."

I realized that she might be teasing. "What for?"

Meeghan shrugged. "Who knows? Such things come in handy."

She waved, and they drove off, her hair blowing out behind.

I stood at the point where two roads meet, looking at the house, so simple and cheerful on one side, the other taking on an air of mystery in the early dusk.

Locusts shrilled in the nearby trees. A mourning dove gave its last crooning call of the day. The katydids began their endless argument: Yes, she is; no, she isn't. She is; she isn't.

Which of them was right? I didn't really want to know.